LIFE

is unpredictable, you might have plans for your self
but the universe might have other plans for you.

Ahmed Alnajem

ISBN: Hardcover   978-1-5437-4302-9
               Softcover   978-1-5437-4301-2
               eBook   978-1-5437-4303-6

To order additional copies of this book, contact
Toll Free 800 101 2657 (Singapore)
Toll Free 1 800 81 7340 (Malaysia)
orders.singapore@partridgepublishing.com

www.partridgepublishing.com/singapore

Slip
Dream

Ahmed Alnajem

PARTRIDGE

Sometimes we all get the feeling that something is not over yet, a situation that needed closure which wasn't going to end any time soon, and it keeps you wondering, when will this ever be done?, will I be able to have peace of mind any time soon?, I have been carrying this feeling around for some time now, it's been like a weight on my shoulders since my teen days, and every day things kept adding up to it, Sometimes we miss minor details in a situation and end up on the short end of the stick, and that is never a good thing, when a man ends up behind bars, he has nothing more than time to think about what he did and where did he go wrong, and would you believe that all of this started years ago because of a simple smile, and what happened after was going to change my life forever.

My name is Derek Jackson, my friends call me DJ and this short story goes a bit like this, I was the first son, dad and mom were the oldest of their siblings in both families, so I was like a prince, I had all the attention from everyone around me, I did good at school and in sports as well, I got a diploma in mechanical engineering and had lots of fun as a party DJ on the weekends and part time radio DJ on the week days to make some income when I was in college, I can really say that I made a name for myself in everything I got my head into, I love working with my hands, I'm smart enough to take care of myself and the people I love.

We were not a rich family but we had respect of all who knew us, I wanted to complete that circle and become rich, but I got kicked out of the radio coz of someone else's fault, after I got my diploma I worked at a government job as a mechanic and in short I hated it, so I left that job, My hunger for getting rich got me started on moving hash around, I earned the name chocolate man since my radio days, I did this for close friends only at first then things got a bit bigger, I decided to earn some cash off it after I got kicked out from my radio job, I had a cool list of classy clients, I took care of them & they took good care of me.

Party djing wasn't paying as well as it was, plus I got tired of carrying my equipment's around, which lead me to street racing and I took to it like a duck to water, felt like there was a space waiting for me to fill, When it comes to street racing I'm what you call a lone wolf, I rome the streets alone, no crew, I started on tuning my friends cars, soon I got the reputation of being the man to see for a low budget or a full car tuning and upgrading service, so some more money started to pure into my pocket, but still wasn't enough. I love cars, party life, women and money, but the story doesn't start here ..

By luck I came across a 2002 Porsche 911 body no engine or transmission, I bought it from a guy that was leaving town for a small amount of cash, and that was my outlaw project car, I took my time to make it work, I started with an Ls3 Chevy small block engine And and an original manual transmission, then I started fishing for 50 - 100 $ races by acting naive when I get challenged while cruising, I saved my winnings and kept on upgrading it bit by bit until I ended up racing for real money or pink slips uptown where the rich boys with deep pockets are, and some of them pay good money to keep their cars, now I call the shots on any challenge I get, this car payed for itself and me .

I kept adding new upgrades to it as I went, taking it from an innocent looking car to a level 2 semi-pro street bad boy,that means that I can drive it around and race it too,I took it from a shell to a working car to a sleepr to a street racers nightmare, I gave it a wider body, bigger wider wheels & tires for better traction, I reduced the weight by taking out whatever I can do without, added an exhaust system, adjustable suspension, ecu, a full engine and transmission upgrade, whatever it took to make this ride a real street beast, still it had an a/c and a cool sound system, I made a name for myself with it & some cash as well on the black top, I got many offers to sell it but I just couldn't, I felt a connection between me & that car that I just couldn't break.

I did my best not to create enemy's but instead I had gained some peoples envy & jealousy, they wanted to take what I had or destroy it, whatever cash I Made I invested in up to date equipment's and tolls for my workshop, to make it bigger and better, some went towards my family, and the rest I keps for my self, I saved enough to buy some second hand gym equipment for my personal use and creat a small living space at the workshop.

One day this chick roles into town her name was ruby, she was looking to make some cash and a name for herself on the black top, she won some races, lost a few and ended up owing money to the wrong people, and like a knight on a white horse Kevin Artmn stepped in and bought her out, and added her to his crew, racing her to pay her dept and gave her a job at his auto parts shop too, you can tell that Kevin had his eyes on her but he wasn't her type for some reason, women the biggest mystery in the universe, any other girl in her shoes would be all over Kevin for what he did but not MS .Ruby, I wonder why ?! .

I would have stepped in to save her but Kevin made the move before I did, Ruby was worth it, but a few bad decisions in this town can make you sink like the titanic, still there was something mysterious about her, she looked a bit too clean for a street racer, for instance she wears nice comfortable sport shoes most of the time when other chicks wore high heels.

And did I mention that Kevin was a bit of a spoiled brat, he comes from a rich family with power and the right connections, he has a college degree and doesn't need to work for what he wants, Kevin likes street racing, a dirty racer that thinks that street rules don't apply to him or he can make his own rules, owns a car parts shop selling used and new parts, he was on my chocolate list but I had to cut him off, I couldn't trust him much, and to be on my list you have to learn to keep your mouth shut about where you get your chocolate from, safety comes first and discretion is the name of the game .

Both of us carry old battle scars from each other from our school days, he gave me 4 stiches in my left eye brow and 3 stiches in my chin, I gave him a broken arm and a broken nose for his best friend and knocked out a couple of teeth for his other friend, it was self-defense on my side, I got cornered by these three guys, all that coz he saw his younger sister Kelly smiling at me, we were all in the same school, she was a cheerleader, it was the schools track day and I just won first place in 100 meter dash .

After that fight I was transferred to another school, his dad George Artmn used his influence and got my dad fired from his old job, so my dad took his savings and opened up the garage where I do my work now and moved us up out to the other side of town, not the nice side to add to that, just to keep us away from trouble, after a while Kelly and I crossed paths, turns out that she still remembers me, and guys it's true girls do like scars and chocolate no need to explain what went down shortly after, but Kevin doesn't know anything about that, my dad warned me about getting tangled up with Kevin and his family again so I left it all behind me and got on with my life, but I don't think Kevin ever did.
I started a small racing gathering a while ago, I called it the street king fest, where racers get to find out who's the king of the street once a year, if you win you earn the respect, get the cash, bragging rights and wear the crown for the whole year until the next event, it was a cool gathering that grew over time from illegal street racing to a legalized full scale racing event with sponsors and the whole nine yards, racers from out of town started to join are little event, we had it going on, the ladies the music the food it was a 3 days and nights blow out where I get to make some real cash.

A few weeks before this event begins you start to feel the vibe rising, everyone is getting ready for it, shops bring out all the new parts, racers spending money on buying parts, tuning and testing their cars, fixing every little detail to make their rids ready for the challenge, I forgot to mention that first place this year gets 50 thousand big ones cash plus a 30% discount until the next race from the shop of his choice, second and third place get 10 thousand and the same discount from the shop of their choice so it was well worth the effort, it was a win for all .

lately there has been a few car thefts going on, certain racers got their cars stolen after winning a few street races, tension was raising around town, coz the cars simply disappear without a trace, someone was up to no good, one night at my garage I heard a sound, someone was snooping around, I thought it was a stray cat or a dog but to my surprise guess who it was.....

Yea Ms. perfect herself Kevin's toy girl ruby, she showed up uninvited sneaking that fabulous booty in my workshop, it was late, the shop was closed everybody had left and I was doing some final touch ups on a car that should be picked up next morning, the car was parked at the workshops exit gate, a blind spot at the back of the garage behind the office.

Now at the time there were a few cars in the garage getting tuned for racers that want to compete in the street king fest, and just like a doctor my clients trust me to keep a secret, what's under the hood stays between the garage and the car owner, if a client shows up to check on his ride he has to call before walking in, so all other car hoods are down until he or she leaves, some of my clients don't even want others to know where they get their cars done, so we might have to cover those cars, yea it's that bad sometimes, anyway me and Ms. perfect never officially met, I've been to a few of her races, we mostly look at each other from a distance, but never a hi or hello. Ruby is in her early to mid-20's about 5,5', nice coca cola figure, you can say that she would be a v6 turbo body chick, cool personality, she has that Latin beauty, with short hair beautiful light brown eyes, yea I checked her out real good and I think she knows it, but still I kept my distance coz of you know who .

And as she was going around checking the cars, I stepped into the office to look at her from the window, lights were dim so she couldn't see me, I looked under the deck at the garage cam monitor and saw a car outside that drove and parked across the street from the garage and turned off its lights, I didn't turn on the alarm yet coz I was working, so now ruby thinks that she was so slick coz she broke into one of the windows and got in without triggering the alarm.

The cars we had in the garage at the time had their engines mostly dismantled waiting for parts, so nothing special was going on yet, I gave her a few moments to wonder around until she got to the middle of the garage, as she had her back to me and checking under the hood of one of the cars I made my move, walked slowly and quietly until I was right behind her, the view was very tempting specially with those jeans on.

I pulled out my phone took a snap shot of that amazing behind, she jumped when she saw the flash, she bumped her head on the engine cover, she turned around to find me standing there with a devilish smile on my face, I asked very politely :

-Me- can help you miss...
Ruby she said, and had that that wild cat seductive look in her eyes, and then she said...
-Ruby-I've seen you around they call you coco right?
-Me-Mr. Chocolate man to you.
-Ruby-Mr. Chocolate man hmm, Kevin told me about you, he stole your girl and you still hate him for it.
-Me-is that what he says?!! (And I smiled!), just so you know nobody takes anything from me unless I don't want it, it's that simple, that girl chose to go to Kevin coz she had something planed in her mind .
-Ruby-ok I get it, so is this your place?
-Me-it wouldn't make any difference if it was mine or not, you're still trespassing, now tell me why are you here and who sent you...?
-Ruby- I came to check out the comptetion, I need to play my cards right if I want to win in the street king fest, I got to buy myself out of that hell whole.
-Me-is that right.... listen, I don't want to lose my boys trust in me and my business coz of people like you, lucky for you there wasn't anything worth seeing yet, I'm going to let you go this time with a warning, never sneak up in here like this ever again, call before you get here everybody knows this, now if your car needs tuning you can bring it here if you got the cash, but from what I see your car has enough power, the problem is the way you drive.
-Ruby-what??!!!, there's nothing wrong with the way I handle my car.
-Me-take my word for it sweety, it's the way you drive, plus I think someone followed you here, any idea who it might be?
-Ruby-no I came alone.
-Me-come with me.
I took her back to the office to take a look at the monitors.
-Me-that car.
-Ruby-no clue.
-Me-you better be telling the truth.
-Ruby-I swear I don't know.
-Me-ok, you can leave same way you came in, and we'll finish this conversation later.

I took her phone number and stood there watching her leave, that girl can claim like a monkey, I walked back to the front gate to check who it was out side, and to my surprise it was amber !!, wow this must be kevin's ladies night at my place, so I walked up to her to see what's up, when she saw me coming she got out of the car took a couple of steps to the back of car and sat on the trunk with a bottle of beer in her hand and said hey handsome how is it hanging ? .

(Amber peril) and I have a bit of history, a sweet girl with a kind heart and a hard head, she has been on the streets since she was about 17, her mother is spending time behind bars, lone girl no brothers or sisters, her step dad tried to take advantage of her, and her mom went to jail coz of what she did to him to protect her child, she was sent to live with her biological father, but she ran away after a short time, she ended up working for Cesar my greens and hash supplier and street racer too, the smoothest Latino in the big apple, I meet her through him she was one of his delivery girls she was around 20 at that time, she has deep blue eyes that can take you in a deep trance if you stare at them for too long and a body like Sofia Vergara with natural blond hair, and coz she didn't have much to do she started hanging out with us for a while, she helped me with organizing 2 fests, cool girl trust worthy and dependable, always looking for the next best thing, she finished high school before her mom got locked up, I tried to get her to go to college but she didn't feel like it yet as she said !.

chasing an easy life she met Kevin on a delivery one time, she had the notion that she can have him for herself, she couldn't see that he was a spoiled brat self-centered psycho and a smart one too and he liked what he saw, now she can't decide what to do, she couldn't tame that kid, and this other chic Tina Grey who was the girl friend for one of the guys in Kevin's crew is hitting hard on Kevin and pushing every one else away to keep Kevin all to her self after her boy friend went to jail, which meant amber can be on the curve sooner than she thinks.
-Me-hey blondie how you doing' Hun?
-Amber-hey babe, ooh I've been better.
she turned around and pulled out a bag of weed, that's when I saw some markings on her back that looked like a belt or something like that, and it was fresh, so I said :

-Me-I hate to say I warned you.

-Amber-oh you saw that? oh that's nothing, it's one of those leather fetish things with masks and whips you know that S & M shit !, Kevin went nuts after he saw 50 shades of grey I guess, I can manage him when he drinks or gets high but when he sniffs that white powder shit things get out of hand, he comes up with these weird ideas and sometimes I have to role with it, hell I even tried to get him to knock me up but it didn't work, maybe coz of the shit he's using, I think he's shooting blanks I guess.

Then she started to role a joint so I said

-Me-hey are you crazy, rolling out in open now??!!

-Amber-what come on, let's chill like we use too, just me and you some music, just like the old days.

-Me-it's late and I got a car to finish for a costumer to pick up tomorrow morning.

-Amber- it's almost 11 pm and you Hun are a night crawler so the night is still young for you, ok you work and I'll watch then we can smoke ok .

-Me- you know I can't let you inside the garage.

-Amber-ok I'll wait upstairs, I'll watch some tv, play a game or something til you finish.

-Me-does he know you're here?

-Amber-no hun he's out on the boat with Tina and some of his crew, won't be back any time soon.

-Me-ok, but you're not sleeping over ok?

-Amber-ok...fine, what you got a girlfriend now??

-Me-ha ha, very funny, drive your car to the backdoor park it behind the container.

needless to say she had something cocking in the back of her head, and she wasn't going to let it go, she came inside, we smoked one and talked a bit, I called for Chinese food, and went back to working on the car, by the time the food got here I was almost done, I covered the car and the time was past midnight, I went upstairs and guess what she's half naked wearing one of my t-shirts and fell asleep on my sofa bed!.

I tried to wake her up but she was way out cold I think she needed to remember how it felt in the old days, so I covered her with a blanket, then had a shower and ate my dinner, sure as hell I wasn't going to leave her alone here, so I looked the door and slept on the sofa bed next to her, it wasn't easy to let that beauty go to waste but I like it like Gollum said (give it to us raw and wriggling).

Amber is a morning person, she can't help but wake up early, it's nice to wake up to some affection once in a while and the smell of fresh coffee, and before I opened my eyes I heard her whisper to herself (god I was so stupid to leave this place!),I opened my eyes to a smiling face and a hot cup of coffee in her hand, I pretended that I didn't hear what she whispered, I got up kissed her on the cheek, thanked her for the coffee, went to wash up, brushed my teeth, came out as she was getting dressed up, I couldn't help but stop and stair, she turned around, smiled then said (you know that you can still have this anytime you want Hun), at that moment she took my breath away with her smile, all I can do was smile, play it cool but on the inside I was revving at 9000 rpm .

I put my clothes on, and as I was drinking my coffee, she came up and kissed my lips gently, then she said you still taste good with coffee, we had a few laughs about the old days, it was almost 8.30 am and she had to leave before my workers get her, I unlocked the door and walked her to her car and watched her drive away back to Kevin's place, on her way back she stopped at the doughnut shop just as Kevin was passing by on his way back from the boat party.

he saw her coming out of the shop, she saw him and waved with a smile as he turned around and parked behind her car, she went up to him :
-Amber- hey babe good morning.
-Kevin- hey sunshine, aren't you a bit far away from home?
-Amber- am never far away from you babe, I woke up early and I wanted to make you a nice breakfast, then I remembered your favorite doughnuts so I came to get you some.
-Kevin- it's like you read my mind, what would I do without you sunshine.
-Amber- how was your night?
-Kevin- ooh it was crazy, I'll tell you about it over breakfast.
-Amber- ok sweaty by the time you take a shower your breakfast will be on the table.
-Kevin- ok sunshine I'll see you at home, drive carefully.
-Amber- I will, take care babe.

All the time when they were talking Kevin was checking her out, the doughnut shop wasn't too far away from my garage so he had his suspicions.

with that aside, later that morning I went out to get something to eat and I got a phone call from an old friend of mine a party caterer Jeff Holland about a party in L.A next Saturday, so I said sure why not, how can you refuse having some fun plus getting paid for it, it was some rich girls party and he recommended me as a DJ, I needed some time out any way, It's Monday so I have a few days to take care of some business.

after breakfast I went back to the garage and took a last look at the car that was received by another satisfied costumer, I made a few calls to check about some parts for some cars we had waiting, I called the a/c company to send someone to do the annual check for the garage's central air coolers, I have to keep my workers cool and the cars cooler, by noon we had nothing much to do, I gave my boys the rest of the day off, I brought my ride inside for a cleanup, by 2 pm I was done, I got in it drove home for some of moms cooking and a nap coz I had a night race I have to attend on the other side of town.

there's no place like home, I just can never have enough of that feeling, it's like this is the only place where you can really feel your body mind and soul just do a group hug, this is one way to but it into a vision, as soon as I walk through the door I feel relaxation, tranquility and peace, I just can't get enough of this luxury, after lunch I slept like a baby and woke up around 7 pm and spent some time with the family then we had a good dinner meal, by 10 I was all set for my drive across town, got in my ride and got on my way, I had to stop for gas and a snack, and as I was leaving the gas station I got suddenly blocked by a patrol car, and not just any patrol car it's the hottest one yet, a modified mustang cobra driven by no other than Jake Henley.

Kevin's childhood friend the one I knocked out a couple of his teeth out in the school fight we had, a street racer turned cop, with the help of Kevin's dad but still races on the down low, he has a heavy foot on the gas when he drives, loves American muscle cars, a crocked cop does some dirty work for Kevin or his dad some times.

he gives me a long look with a wicked smile then did that I got my eyes on you gesture, I smiled back and pointed at my teeth same ones I knocked out for him, I guess he didn't like my move, so he drove away in a smoke cloud.

after about a 30 minute drive I got to the race, I saw that things were cooking, I'm here coz of the car I was working on last night, I want to see how well it runs, but my surprise was to see that the cars owner was racing one of Kevin's crew, then it hit me, maybe ruby wasn't telling the truth after all, I decided to play it cool and go with the flow, everyone was there, I parked my car and put in a bet on the car I tuned, I met a few friends and checked out some of the local honeys, I turned around and there was Ms. Ruby, so I sent her a message, I sent her the picture I took of her butt last night, she took her phone out saw the picture and giggled, she started looking around but she didn't notice me, she replied

-Ruby-are you some kind of pervert?
-Me-it's called evidence sweet cheeks...
-Ruby-lol, sweet cheeks ha! Then you must like what you saw.
-Me- you need to keep your eyes on the drag race, your friend in the red car handles it just like you do, puts his foot on the gas and hopes to win, the more horse power the better, the guy in the green car is more technical, his car is more of power to weight ratio, he knows his car and he becomes a part of it, man and car in perfect harmony
p.s - Are those the same pants you had on last night?? ttyl.
-Ruby-how do you know all that?? Where are you? Hello!
now the race is about to start, cars are lined up, bets are sealed and waiting for the final word from the road scots ahead, cars revving their engines, the scots send back the all clear, everyone is on edge, the race starer hits the light and they jump off the start line.

lots of smoke from the red car as he jumps half a car ahead, the green car pulls off a much smoother start, 2nd gear and they are still at the same distance from each other but the red car is still burning rubber, it's sending too much power to the rear wheels, the green car starts to pull next to it at 3rd gear, by 4th gear and a nitrous boost the green car has managed to win by a car length at the end of the quarter mile.

After things cooled down Kevin turns around to this shady guy standing in the back and nods to him, it must have been a sign, what for?, I don't know, it was so cool for me, I feel like a proud father every time a car I tunned wins a race, I collected my money and got in my car rolled a joint for the road, and smoked it on the way home listening to a reggae track, a perfect end to a perfect day.

((((((Tuesday))))))
next morning I woke up to my phone ringing, I picked it up it was ruby, asking to meet me at a cafe at a nearby strip mall, so I got up took a shower, I but my clothes on and gave mom a morning kiss on my way down stairs, said good morning to my dad and asked if they wanted anything before I leave, it was another beautiful morning, and to see all my family in good health is a blessing from god.

I got in my car and ten minute later I was at the cafe, I saw her sitting outside having her coffee, she looks even better in the sun, she was wearing a light blue torn jeans shorts and a light white shirt, I can see her pink braw under it from where I am, I knew two things, one she still is a girly girl still InTouch with her inner child, two she will try to manipulate me into doing something for her, I got out of my car and walked into the coffee shop got me a cappuccino a muffin and a snake for later, then I came up behind her and stood there for a sec admiring the view from the top,she was facing the sun so she didn't see my shadow, I said good morning sweet cheeks, she smiled, looked back at me.

-Ruby-good morning, you are a sneaky one aren't you, how was your night?
-Me-profitable, too bad I can't say the same for you guys.
-Ruby-yea, Kevin got so mad he punched the drivers light out, coz he wasted a lot of money on that car, plus the guy cost him his bet, he's just lucky he didn't shoot him.
-Me-good old Kevin, so what did you bring me her for, other than the view?
-Ruby-I don't want to end up like that guy, and you seem to know a few tricks.
-Me-so...??
-Ruby-teach me how to squeeze the juice out of my ride.
And she said that in a seductive way.
-Me-is that what you brought me her to talk about?

-Ruby- uh huh...
-Me-hmm...I'll get back to you on that, now I got a go to work.
-Ruby-wow you don't waste time do you, so is that a yes?
-Me-it's a definite maybe, you said there's nothing wrong with your driving.
-Ruby-I know I said that, but I think I need to learn some new moves.
-Me-let's see what you got first.
-Ruby-ok fine, when??
-Me-I'll let you know, see you when I see you.

I left her sitting there wondering if her beauty and charm had worked on me, I got in my car and drove to the shop to see what we have to finish today, lucky for me I got there just in time, caught up with the spare parts guy and two of my workers just came in to help me move the parts off the truck, we got some of the parts to get a couple of the cars done, a few drivers came in to get their cars tuned but I'm not taking in any cars this week, a couple of hours later the A/C guys came in for the annual checkup, that's good coz the weather was heating up, after lunch time we were almost done with the cars we had and some more parts arrived, now I'm hoping to clear the shop by Thursday or Friday coz I need a day to chill for the L.A party, now it's closing time, it was a good day at the shop no surprises.

I closed up shop and went home, I had my shower then had dinner and a short nap, I woke up a couple of hours later with Ruby on my mind, something was telling me to see what this girl is up to, I sent her a message saying (let me know if your free tonight), at the time Ruby was with Kevin and a couple of guys at the garage that Kevin deals with, these days Kevin tries to keep Ruby under his watchful eyes where ever he goes and that drives Tina crazy, little does she know that Ruby is not interested in Kevin at all, still she tries her best to keep Kevin all to herself, she thinks that she managed to get Amber out of the picture now it's Ruby's turn to disappear, 30 minutes later she replies (at the tuning shop with the boys, be out in 15 minutes, what's up ??), I asked her to let me know when she's out coz I wanted to take a look under her hood .... Yes I said it.

I went downstairs to get a cup of coffee, by the time I was half way through it I got a message from Ruby saying I'm out, where are you, I told her to meet me at a 24/7 grocery shop near my house, I walked to the place and a few minutes later she arrived, she was driving a purple Camaro, she turned off the car and popped the hood, when I saw the engine I knew it, I worked on this engine before, last I heard about this car it was in the police impound !!.

I took my phone out, turned on the flash light, I looked around and took a picture of the chassis number and just kept looking around, after a minute I said ok take me for a ride, we drove into the city and as we were chatting I sent a message to a friend of mine that worked at the police impound to check the chassis number for me, I remember this engine but on a deferent car, deferent color and had a manual transmission, the car I'm in right now is an automatic.

a few minutes later I got the reply saying that the original Camaro is still in the L.A police impound, but a while ago the engine was taken out of it and the chassis number too, still needs a complete rear half coz it was almost totaled in a police chase, and the original owner Carlos is still in jail, so this car has been built for Ruby but not registered to her name and how did she get her hands on that engine, something doesn't smell right, as usual I kept my mouth shut.

now we are in the down town area, I really wanted to see how she handles herself with this car, so luck serves me well, we found some kids in a nice ride at a traffic light, I looked ahea and street was almost empty then I turned at them and pulled out a 100 $ and waved it at them, I smiled and said get to the next light before we do and this will be yours, he saw that a girl was driving I guess he thought it's easy money, by listening to his car I can tell it was a bit like street racer semi pro car, so we're good.

he starts revving his engine, I looked at her and said don't make me lose my money now, she looked over to other car then smiles and starts revving too, waiting for the light to turn green felt like forever to her a couple more seconds and she might have started to sweat, not a typical racer attitude, she was too tense, then instead of keeping the gear on D and keeping one foot on the gas and the other on the brakes, she kept revving with gear on neutral, the light went green and she pulled that gear shift down hard, I felt the hit in the transmission, a few more times like this and it's going to shatter, the car did a massive burnout, tiers smoking like crazy, lucky for her she had street slick tiers.

after a couple of second the car got a grip on the tarmac and took off, I
see the rpm going all the way into the red then shifting to the next gear,
the engine was screaming like a beast out of hell, the other car was a stick
shift, both have almost equal performance but the other guy was a bit of
a slow shifter, it was really close, We won by half a car, maybe if the other
guy knew how to deal with his car a bit better I might have lost my money.

this girl has heart and nothing else, no street race knowledge what so ever,
I kept my money, she was over the moon with this win, singing hoop there
it is, a minute later she cooled down, but now we have to skip town before
the cops show up, took the nearest exit back to my neighbourhood, at the
time when we were out a crew has located last night's winner car and jacked
it using a fake garbage truck that can open on the side with 2 hydraulic
arms with brackets and straps, they just pick up the car bring it in, close the
hatch and drive away, get in the car later, smart, smooth and time saving.

on the way back this girl was talking about how she kicked that kids ass and
how badass her car is, and the other guy didn't have a chance, basically she
was high of her win, I asked her to drop me off at the same place we met,
good thing it wasn't a long drive, when we arrived and I was getting out of
the car she asked me what do I think about the race.
-Me-I think your car has a short life span 2 to 4 races max.
-Ruby-what do you mean??
-Me-I mean you are killing your car with the way you race it, I don't know
how long you were racing, coz I find it hard to believe that you ever did
before you showed up here, and whoever tuned your car is an idiot.
-Ruby-I was tense coz you were with me, am use to being alone when I race.
-Me-ooh so is that it really!!(I was just being sarcastic).
-Ruby-give me another chance to show how I role with it when am in the
groove.

I smiled, coz I knew she's was trying to screw with my mind again, and
she said that while she was leaning towards me to hit me with a view of
you know what.
-Me-care to put some cash on that.
-Ruby-for real?

-Me- I bet you can't win your next race even if I let you pick who you want to race, and if you win I might hook you up with a few pointers and a tune up for your car plus the cash.
-Ruby-and if I lose?

-Me-I take your money, no tune up, and no pointers, deal?
-Ruby-how much?
-Me-1000$
-Ruby-I don't have that kind of cash now.
-Me-I got to go home now, think about it, we both know that you don't need that kind of pressure right, good night sweet cheeks.
-Ruby-good night and stop calling me sweet cheeks!!
She screamed that as I was walking away with a big grin on my face, I was trying to make her change her mind and push her away.

She drove slowly next to me and asked

-Ruby-what if I don't have the money?
-Me-I looked in her eyes then said I'll take your wheels.
she didn't say a word and just drove away.

((((Wednesday))))
next morning I woke up to a message from Ruby saying (good morning, ok fine you are on, who am I racing?), now I don't know what this girl it trying to prove, but I know she's old enough to decide for herself, now I don't know if she actually came up with the cash or not, any way I got my morning started as usual, then went to the workshop to finish the work we have on the last few cars left, a couple of hours later Shawn the guy that owned the green car I tuned calls me asking to meet, I said sure, I met him outside the garage, he showed up with a sad look on his face.

-Me-hey man what's up, why the long face??
-Shawn-hey bro, my car got stolen last night man, after all the time and money I put in to it.
-Me-damn the green lantern!!! Sorry to hear that man, how did that happen?
-Shawn-it was parked outside the house didn't drive it into the garage coz I wanted to wash it in the morning, but when I woke up it was gone, that car was my baby, I built it from a shell, 2 years of hard work just vanished.

-Me-I understand how you feel bro, did you go to the police yet?

-Shawn-yea gave them all the details, they gave me the usual (we will do our best to find your car sir) crap.

-Me-you know this has been going on for a while now, I don't know for sure how many but it's almost a dozen or more just in the past couple of months.

-Shawn-yea man, I noticed a pattern, most of them are fine-tuned race winners or exotics, and I don't know how they bypass the tracking systems.

-Me-I don't know bro, but if there's anything I can do anytime just let me know ok man.

-Shawn-yea thanks man, peace.

-Me-be safe bro.

it breaks my heart to see someone like Shawn depressed, somebody needs to put an end to this, I got back to my work and the day just flew by like a bullet, I had two cars in the shop, now I'm down to one, the last car just need a couple of parts installed then we can do an engine check and tune it, that means by tomorrows closing time my shop will be empty, that clears Friday for me to make a few phone calls and get myself ready for the L.A party, Ruby has messaged me about 3 or 4 times asking about what's going on, where are you, is the race tonight, I sent her a message when I was done and asked her to meet me at the same place tomorrow night.

closing time and I'm craving for something sweet, I stopped by the doughnut shop nearby and ran into Mr. bad boy wanna be (Kevin) with a couple of his boys, so out of being polite I said hey Kev

-Kevin-hey it's the chocolate man, long times no see, how you been?.

-Me-I'm good can't complain, just doing what I do, are you going to race in the fest this time ?, you know it's within a few of weeks from now.

-Kevin-funny you should ask it just happiness that I will this time.

-Me-ooh yea, that is a surprise.

-Kevin-yea got a set of wheels that's going to blow your mind, something old school, real muscle.

-Me-ah ha....

-Kevin-big and beautiful, I'm going to take this fest by a storm.

-Me-hey you never know, it might be your lucky fest.

-Kevin- I don't need luck, I got this, it's in the bag son (starts laughing and hi fiving his boys)

-Me-well well aren't we so full of ourselves, stay cool guys, peace for now (as I left the shop)
-Kevin-cool as ice and twice as nice, see you on the black top.

That boy had something up his sleeve, I noticed that Kevin has a new crew member, an electronics whiz kid Bruce change, he goes to the same school as my younger brother Darrell, he's around 15-16 years old, half Asian from his father's side, the best description would be a cool nerd, but what the hell is he doing with Kevin ? .

I kept thinking about it all the way back to my house, and over the dinner table I asked my brother Darrell if he knew Bruce and if he has any idea why is he hanging with Kevin, he said he's cool with Bruce, about a month ago he saw Kevin outside the school talking to his baby cousin which Bruce has a crush on, she introduced Bruce to Kevin, since then this guy has been showing off some bling and other stuff, that was very interesting, after that I made one more phone call to set up a race for ruby tomorrow night and got the approval, so I called it a night and went to bed early.

(((Thursday)))
I woke up early and went to the work shop coz I have a couple of guys coming to pick up their cars, I just have to put the final touches on them, after lunch time the cars were gone, and I'm free, I gave the guys the next 2 days off coz they earned it, i had some time to make a few phone calls to start the arrangements for the fest, I called a few local business owners, sponsors, we got to start building this from the ground up, got to start making my money, got lots more to do over the next 2 weeks, that's why I stop everything to fucos on making it bigger and better.
closing time and I gotta get home coz I got a crazy date later tonight, I sent Ruby a text (if you still want to do this meet me at the same place as last time at 11 pm, better have cash), I wish I could have seen her face when she opened the text, I got home and after a warm shower and a hot meal with the family, I took a nice nap untill it was time to move out, something told me I need to be on my tows tonight, and black coffee had the answer for that, for some reason I felt like driving tonight, I got into my outlaw mobile, and as I was approaching the place I saw ruby's car, oh yea she's already there, I came next to her and rolled down my window, she was smiling, a smile of girl with a plan,

-Me-hey you, are you ready for this.
-Ruby-I was born ready.
-Me- alright, let's hit the road, follow me but not too close.
-Ruby-lead the way.

we drove to the Asian side of town, port side near the docks, home of the
Ronin crew, the terror of the far east, with their own set of rules, I knew a
few of those boys, some good some bad some just pure crazy extremists,
so when I told my guy Yoshi that ruby is going to pick the car she wants to
race he said the owner of the car she picks will pick what kind of race, drag,
circuit, drift, sprint or follow the leader, by the time we got there things
were cocking, we parked our cars and exchanged greetings with the boys,
I introduced ruby to them and told her time to take your pick.
The guys are standing next to their cars, some of the cars look innocent but
fully armed under the hood, it took her quite a while to make up her mind
but finally she did, the car she picked belonged to Tommy jinn, he looked
at her car he knew that it was tuned for a short race so he said circuit race,
ruby almost fainted when she heard that.

-Ruby-what!!
-Me-their turf their rules, chill out, I think you have a good chance of
catching him.
-Ruby-you are joking right??
-Me-no for real, keep your mind on the game and your eyes on the road,
just don't crash your car ok.
-Ruby-I hate you...
-Me-hate is such a powerful word, my advice to you is to keep your gear on
Drive at the starting line, left foot on the brake and right foot on the gas
and don't go full throttle on the start, push the engine up to about 3000
rpm then punch it when you get of the starting line and the rest is up to
you, focus, stay cool go get him kid.
race time, cars to the start line, destination is set in the GPS, ruby is getting
that feeling again, she's sweating bullets for real this time, she turned
around at me, I looked her straight in the eye and said softly (you can do
this) with a smile, she read my lips and smiled so I winked at her, she took
a deep breath and looked ahead, she saw the starting light and boom she
shoot like a bullet off the line, you can tell that this is the first time she felt
her cars true power, she screamed (wooooooow), and for a few seconds she

forgot about the other racer coz she left him behind her staring at her tail lights, it was a perfect start of the line for her for the first time.

by the time she woke up from that high they reached the first turn, she slowed down getting into it then punched it hard, the car went nuts tiers smoking hard, she had her jump but now the other car is catching up, we lost sight of them after that turn, but we can still hear them, I think she started to figure out how powerful her car is, so now she's feeling the car and connecting with it, with every passing second, with every turn she's more into it, she managed to keep the lead for the first lap,but still Tommy was right on her tail, Ruby had the power, Tommy had the street knowledge and he's not going down easy, I guess Tommy took some time to actually study Ruby on the first lap, you got to respect those guys.

then Tommy just went kamikaze on the start of the second lap, he hit the nitrous coming down the straight line as they were passing us, throwing his car ahead of Ruby and drifting into the turn takin the lead, ruby has one chance to win this, a straight road near the ship yard, if she can get in it the right way she might manage to pull him back, now this lap takes about 2 minutes give or take a few seconds, during the first lap someone had called the police and reported a race going on, the nearest patrol car around was officer Jake Henley in the mustang or the road beast as he calls it, so by the time they started their second lap he was actually there, and saw them as they passed by.

well you know the rest, we heard the sirens and turned around and saw Ruby and Tommy coming out of the last turn drifting like crazy with the red and blue lights behind them, we are seeing this like it was in slow motion, by the time they got to that turn ruby was not too far ahead of tommy, she actualy managed to catch tommy but he managed to bull her back again by drifting into the last turn, now it's not really clear who was leading from where we stood there as they hit the straight coming towards us, that's when tommy went into scramble mood and took the first turn to freedom, ruby on the other hand kept coming as we started hearing more sirens, it's now or never so I told Yoshi (we'll finish this later peace bro).

I jumped in my car and turned on my police scanner to hear what's going on, I had to rush it out of there, coz officer Jake would love to get his hands on my car for real, he wanted to buy it for so long but I told him it's not for sale, I started my run as ruby was getting closer, when Jake saw my car, he got fixed on it, now he wants it more than ever, so bad that he was passing other cars just to get to me.

two police cars blocked the road in front of me, I got on the pavement to get around them, it hurts me to do this to this car but I had to do it, Jake is still on my tail, another police car hits the brakes in front of me so I took the nearest turn out of that street, I put my foot on the gas and boosted out of there but still I'm not alone, suddenly my phone rings, I had my Bluetooth on my ear so I picked up.

-Me-yea....
-Ruby-what can I do to help?
-Me-if you want to help me get this guy off my back.
-Ruby-not right now, I can't catch up with you guys.
-Me-then just get the hell out of here, I'll call you if I want your help.

by now jack has been calling for more cars, I need to stop this guy dead in his tracks, I'm still twisting and turning dodging police cars with him on my tail then I saw my opportunity, I went into the ship yard, I remembered a triangle pavement between the warehouses in that area, I knew I had to stick him in it one way or the other, coz as long as he can see me I won't be able to get away, after a few turns I got rid of all the other police cars, now it's just jack and I, I only have a few minutes before the police helicopter arrives.

I dragged him to my trap, I raced a few times here before and there is a network of short roads between the warehouses that I knew well, it was a dark area not all the street lights there work, but something cought my eye, I think I saw a light in one of the warehouses there as they were closing the door and some cars were in there, now in my car I have installed a rear flash light, much like a camera flash light with a little red light that blinks to grab the attention and then you get a massive flash, like a light bomb, my plan was to get him to come closer and when I'm near the triangle, I'll flash him & move out of the way as simple as that, so his car would get stuck and maybe damage the steering system at least.

as we got closer to the place I stayed right in front of him as we approached the triangle, I held my breath kept my thumb on the flash button on the steering wheel, now just a few more seconds and boom I hit him with it, I moved away and kept looking in my rear view mirror as the mustang wheels went in different direction, with jake's foot still on the gas and the motor was revving like crazy, the airbag shocked poor Jake, he didn't even see it coming.

then I pulled my disappearing act, I took the back road out of the port area, now I really need to hide this car, just make it disappear for a while, so I called Tony a friend of mine who owned a small car paint and vinyl rap shop, the guy was a night owl, works nights mostly, I wasn't too far away, Tony really wanted to rap this car, in his own words (I have a vision for this car), I called him up and told him it's your lucky night, I'll explain it to you when I get there just don't sleep ok, I'll be there shortly, the guy has been waiting for this for a long time now.

by the time I got there it was after 1 am,I drove into the shop, we closed the doors and sat down, I asked him to call me a cab and told him the whole story, and if anybody asks about the car tomorrow, just say that you had this car since yesterday just don't say since what time, I'll come to pick it up on Sunday, you better amaze me bro, use the good vinyl coz I want to keep this paint job after taking it off after a while, take good care of my baby,then he said don't worry man I'll treat her like my girlfriend, somehow I got an image in my mind of him humping the car, I think being close to paint fumes that long can make a man say stuff like that!!.

The cab arrived, I gave the driver the address to the garage coz it was late and I didn't want to disturb my family, on the way I got a message from ruby asking.
-Ruby-where are you, are you ok?
-Me-yes I am thanks for asking.

and I left it at that, I got to the garage, I had a shower and got a microwave meal prepared, and I sat down to eat it, half way through my meal I get another message from ruby saying (I'm outside let me in I need to talk to you), I guess she was driving around and saw the lights, I called her to see what's up ..

-Me- can't this wait until tomorrow?

-Ruby-no, I won't take too much of your time I promise.

-Me-ok, park behind the shop, I'll be there in a minute.

I went down to see what is it, she asked to can come inside so I took her upstairs, as soon as she stepped in she turned around and pulled me and hit me with a long luscious kiss, I thought oh my god (in my mind), she was still on the adrenalin high, then she split my shirt from the neck down, I looked down at my shirt and said

-Me-this was one of my favorite shirts, are you sure that you can handle what comes next??

-Ruby-show me your worst...

I Looked her straight in the eye, and I started growling (in my mind), I went into werewolf mood on that body, it was a wild night.

Friday morning I woke up a bit later than usual, I went straight into the shower, made some fresh coffee then I woke up sleeping beauty, I sat in front of my lap top to check e-mails while having my coffee, she walked up to me kissed me good morning then went to take a shower, those faded glass shower doors finally paid off, I can watch that booty getting wet all day long.

distractions aside, I had to get my stuff ready for Saturday coz am leaving on this evenings flight to L.A, I got a hand bag out started packing some clothes and my cd's, as she got dressed and pored herself a cup of coffee she saw me packing and asked me

-Ruby-how long you going to be away?

-Me-just a couple of days, blow out some steam.

-Ruby-sounds like fun.

-Me-a bit of change from the usual.

she was looking at her phone and found a few messages from Kevin, I guess she wasn't too happy to see those messages,then she said I wish I can come with you but I have to go, let me know when you get back papi, then she kissed me and left, I was speechless, all I did was watch that amazing figure walk away.

A few minutes later I was done with packing and booked my ticket online, it was getting close to lunch time, I drove the shop's pick up back to my house to spend some time with the family, on the other hand Ruby didn't have an easygoing day, until she got to Kevin's shop where she works and

ran into kevin who was in a very integrative mood, he asked her to come
into his office

-Kevin-hey princess, you're a bit late today, how was your night??
-Ruby-ah very eventful, too bad you missed it.
-Kevin-I wouldn't if you would have told me, too bad I had to hear about
it from someone else!
-Ruby-yea what did you hear?
-Kevin-I guess you're lucky that the race ended the way it did, you could've
lost your money or ended up behind bars, I don't know why you make me
worry about you?.
-Ruby-I'm a big girl Kevin, I can take care of myself.
-Kevin-are you out of your fucking mind, you're not ready to deal with
those guys, and you should have told me before you do that.
-Ruby-so now I need your permission? I need to earn some cash to pay you
back, I'm sick and tired of being treated like some pet.
-Kevin-one more thing, did DJ have anything to do with it ?, I know he
was there, is there anything going on that I should know about, like where
were you last night.
-Ruby-he was there when I was talking with Yoshi about the race details,
I had to hide the car somewhere and I took a cab home, happy now, Kevin
I owe you money and nothing else ok, I need to get something to eat, I'll
see you later.

Kevin has been trying to hit that booty for some time now, somehow I don't
see him getting that any time, while he spent his day chewing on himself,
ruby went on a girls day out, beauty salon, spa, shopping, I think her
feminine instinct woke up after last night's events, you know what I mean....

by evening time I was on a plane to the city of angles, got myself set up
with a nice European exotic rental waiting for me outside the airport and
a lavish 5 star hotel suite, I'm here to have some fun remember, it was still
early so I hit the hotels night club for an hour then went up to my room
got a massage, then a meal and to end all that I smoked some green magic
outside on the suite balcony looking at the city lights, a few minutes later I
went to bed for a good night sleep.

Saturday was a beautiful sunny day, a classic L.A morning, I had breakfast in my room while looking at an amazing view outside the window, an hour later I got a location message from Jeff, I got dressed took my music with me jumped in the car and drove to the party place, I got to check the equipments and speakers and set up everything the way I like, the drive was about 30 minutes to a magnificent designer villa up in the hills overlooking the city, Jeff was waiting for me at the entrance, after a few HI's & hello's I followed him inside driving slow and easy, you really have to see the place, some crazy modern art work along the way to the main building I couldn't understand most of it, when we got to the party area I asked Jeff about the place, and he told me it belongs to this rich guy that rents it out most of the year coz he's out of the country most of the time, jeff got me the DJ equipments and the speakers I asked for.

I started putting the speakers around the place, setting up the equipment, by now I'm ready to do a proper sound check, as the music filled the place a hummer limo drove in, Jeff was standing next to me at the time and told me that it's the birthday girl and a few of her friends

(heather pinks) was her name as Jeff was telling me, he knew who's who in this town, he said she was a nobody until a couple of years ago when she met a rich older man on her 21st birthday in a down town bar who became her sugar daddy, the guy is spending money around her like dirt just to keep her happy, now she owns a nice flat thanks to him, she's a bit of an air head but smart enough to keep that guy hooked, this is her 23rd birthday party, and Jeff has been the lucky caterer since then.

Then he threw the guy's name (George Artmn), you need to know this about Kevins dad …
he wasn't as rich as he is all the time, he comes from a humble family, he was full of ambition and his family did whatever they could do to put him into a respectable university, there he met kevin's mom Helen Arlington an elegant young lady with a strong personality, her dad was a business tycoon, after a while they fell in love and shortly after college they got married and George became an employee at Arlington's empire then a manager then the number 1 guy after Helens father passed away a few years after Kevin was born, leaving everything he built to his only daughter.

the hummer doors opened and hot chicks just pureed out, every flavor u like, I'm looking at a month supply of eye candy, they came out of the car dancing and shooting, I think for some of us the party has already started, heather walked up to us and said hi to Jeff and he introduced me to her, the other girls went to the the villa, we were talking about the party program for a few minutes then the girls came out in their swimming suites, some jumped in the pool and others were sun bathing, I guess they didn't call it the city of angels for nothing, after a few minutes I got the general idea about what she wants for her party, then she left to join her friends on the pool side, she said you guys are more than welcome to join us if you like as she smiled and waved bye walked away, Kevin's dads girlfriend no thank you, I better keep my distance.

any way the sound check was good, it's around noon time, I have to get back to my hotel to have lunch and chill for a few hours so I can come back fresh and ready in the evening to get this party pumping til dawn, when I reached my hotel I got a call from a strange number on my phone, the caller asked if I knew a amber peril, I said yes, is she ok?, they told me that she asked them to call me when she was brought to the hospital by ambulance an hour ago and that she has been involved in a domestic home accident, when I asked how is she now, they said she was ok and stable but they had to put her to sleep to rest coz she was in pain, a few broses and a fractured rib but overall she will be fine in a short while, knowing Kevin I knew something wasn't right about this, thank god it's only minor injuries.

after a good lunch and a few hours nap i got up and called room service to hook me up with a club sandwich and a fresh juice, I hit the shower and while getting dressed my food got here, I don't do energy drinks it just doesn't work for me, I remembered to call the hospital to check on Amber and they told me that she's still sleeping, so I asked them to let me know if anything happens, at this time it was starting to get dark, that means I better be on my way to the party,It took me a few minutes to put my clothes on and I was on my way, when almost got to the villa I had to stop for a minute and get out of the car to take a few pictures of the amazing view of the city of angles from above, it's enchanting to look at city lights extending into the horizon.

Then I got back on the road, I got to the front gate and as it opened I saw what they got going on inside, it felt like I was in Ibiza on a summer night, lasers, colored lights, a huge disco ball over the dance floor, multi colored light bubbles scattered around the place, the only thing missing is the music, I can tell it was going to be a crazy night, waiters were putting the last touches on the place, I parked my car and went straight to the DJ's both, I can hear the girls laughing as they're getting ready for the party inside the villa from where i stand, I asked one of the waiters to hook me up with a cup of coffee and bring it over to the DJ both, time for a final sound check and learn how the light system works you know get acquainted with the works.

I was done with my coffee and smoked a joint in the bush behind the DJ both, now people are arriving the place was filling up, I was playing some tracks just to get the party vibe started, heather and the girls were out mingling with people, drinking chatting, then they brought the cake out, the crowd gathered around it and the girls were singing happy birthday to heather, the lights went off when she blew out the candles, just in that instant a spot light was shined on the drive way as a cool convertible red sport coupe drove slowly towards the dance floor with Mr.Artmn in it, he parked it near the dance floor, one of the waiters was waiting there with a wireless mic, I turned the volume up for Mr.Artmn's short speech, heather walked over and stood next to him, she kissed him on the cheek, Mr.Artmn held her close and said ..

-Mr.Artmn- my dearest, my sweet heather, snice I met you about 2 years ago You brought back color in my life, life suddenly had an exciting taste, you take me to another universe when I'm with, your my little world my sweet honey girl, happy birthday sweety I hope you like your gift.

I guess she was surprised to know that her gift was a car, she hit him with a big kiss and started jumping like a 5 year old kid, people were clapping and shouting party, party, and that was my call to get it started, so I dropped the beats on them, we officially went into night club mood, Mr.Artmn and heather walked on to the dance floor as the first couple to start dancing and people got in after them, I was rocking the house with the hottest tracks and I wasn't too away far from the dance floor, and I was doing my best to keep my head down.

I'm wearing a baseball cap and black shades so Mr.Artmn wouldn't notice me, thank god heather had his attention and the girls surrounded them, he didn't stay long he left the dance floor with Heather and went towards the villa, then Heather came back to party and spoke to a few of the girls, then the girls left the dance floor and went inside the villa, I'm just grateful that he didn't see me.

the party went on untill almost dawn, and after every one has left I sat down with Jeff and heather for a light chat while his crew picked up the tables, chairs & party equipment, I got paid with a nice fat envelope, I didn't count the money coz it felt like I got paid extra so it would be rude to do it in front of them, in the middle of our chat Jeff left to check on his workers for a minute while heather kept talking, the girl was a bit drunk so she went on and on, you know how much girls love a good listener so I got a bit greedy, I wanted to know more, time for some green magic, I asked her if it's ok to roll one and she was down with it, now she was already like 70 % drunks and smoking this stuff can go one of three ways with her:
1-the effect goes down south and turns her on.
2-she will keep on talking with more details.
3-she might fall asleep.
So I took my chance with it, lucky for me she kept on talking like a radio science show, turns out that Ms. Heather is a madam in the making, Mr. Arman and a few of his friends enjoy the company of young ladies, and a few of Mr. Artmn's friends were here in the villa tonight having their own little party, and this has opened a door for her to meet some people in high places, like friends of Mr.Artmn and their friends, and she provides something like a private service for these VIP's.

she has a year to go in U.C.L.A and most of her girlfriends are collage girls from different collages, all her school coasts are covered, she has her own place, Mr.Artmn takes good care of her but still he likes to mix it up every once in a while, she doesn't know a lot about Mr.Artmn, he calls her a couple of times or more a month whenever he's in town and the rest of the time she's with friends, about now I'm getting too tired to listen, so I excused myself to leave and she gave me her number and said (call me up whenever you're in town we can hang together) as I walked her to the villa and went to my ride, I drove back to the hotel after great night fun, later I realized that I was given a sword or a shield of some kind, but when or how should I use it still is not clear to me, thank you god.

next day I woke up at around noon, after my shower and a small meal I started packing up my stuff, I got a phone call from the hospital, and to my surprise it was amber on the other side, she told me that she was ok nothing that can't be fixed, I told her that I'm coming back later today and will try to come to the hospital to see her as soon as I get there, I hanged up and finished packing, checked out of the hotel, I got in the car and went back to the airport, I called Jeff to thank him for the hook up then called tony the guy I left my car with on the night of the getaway to see if the car was ready and if he can come pick me up from the airport, and he said ok, I got to the airport returned the car and and I went straight into the plane, hours later we landed and it's starting to get dark, tony was waiting for me, he took me to his shop to see my baby, all the way to the shop he was making my imagination run wild with the new look of the car.

I don't know what this guy was high on when he did this, coz the car looks amazing, a full body cover of black 3d carbon fiber vinyl with a clear vinyl cut of a crawling wolf with bat wings on both sides from the front fender all the way back to the tail light, and an amazing striping job also with clear vinyl on the hood and the trunk, the magic happens when the lights hit the car then you can see all this art work come to life other than that you just see a dark black car, this guy did a great job on this car and took a chunk of my wallet too but it's worth it, I was gitting really hungry for a home meal at the time so I got in my car and drove home just in time for dinner, parked the car inside the garage, and had some great quality family time, it's great to be home,I called the hospital to check on amber but she was already in dream land, knowing that tomorrow is the start of a busy couple of weeks I had to get some sleep, I checked a few e-mails then I went to bed.

next morning I woke up early and after breakfast I took my car back to my work shop,I parked it in the underground parking that I had specially made for it, it's a hydraulic lift that takes the car blew ground, keeps it safe and saves space too, I had to do some checkups and tune ups for the street king fest for some of my workers they want to get their cars ready for the fest too and I do what I can to help, that's why I don't take cars before the fest, I went upstairs to check my e-mails and I was surprised of how many racers want to be apart of the fest, the number keeps getting bigger every time, the hotels and motels were getting fully booked in advance, this fest is really going nation wide, I'm talking about tuners, exotics and muscle cars all in one, my sponsors love it and so do I, coz I get a percentage of what they make.

there is one major difference in street fest we don't do quarter mile runs, it's a half mile race, yes that is the challenge, cars and drivers need to be prepared for it, coz it's not just about horse power, it takes a bigger strategy to run this race, over pushed engines can explode drive trains shatter, that makes knowing when to push your car to the limit a matter of great intelligence, so you need to have a plan, know your car, retune your engine and transmission to get to the finish line, it's not just a race it's more like the politics of races.

I remembered to check on Amber so I called the hospital they said that she is awake, I dropped what I was doing and went to see her, upon my arrival I saw Mrs.Artmn and Kelly leaving the hospital, this woman has an attitude of a first lady and why shouldn't she with a family history like hers who can argue with that, Kelly noticed me but her mom didn't, she waved hello on the down low with a naughty smile on the side as I was getting some rosses for Amber, I smiled back with a simple nod.

I kept on walking until I got to Ambers room, I stopped at a distance for a minutes just to look at her, she looks like she's been in a gang fight, domestic house accident yea right, more of a domestic house beating, I think Kevin is getting more stupid with every passing day, finally I walked in the room, with the rosses in front of my face acting like I'm hiding behind a bush, it made her smile as best a she could, then she said (hey it's nothing that can't be fixed), the amazing part is amber still has a positive attitude and tons of hope, she even made me smile, I hugged her lightly and kissed her on the cheek.

-Me-hey beautiful,you better get well soon you know I need your help to get the fest going.
-Amber-yea I know you can't do it without me.
-Me-I just saw Mrs.Artmn and Kelly leaving the hospital what's up with that?

-Amber-yea they came to see me.

-Me-oh really?

-Amber-yea, Kelly and I became good friends we hang out a lot and turns out that Mrs.Artmn likes me too.

-Me-you're joking right.

-Amber-no it's true, I went to a few of her brunches with Kelly, Kelly asked me to go with her so she won't get bored, I guess some of my magic has rubbed on her mom too.

-Me-yea you do have some magic of your own Hun, I just can't believe it failed to affect Kevin.

-Amber-I think it did, but it's that stuff he uses that makes him unpredictable, actually Mrs.Artmn came to see what I'm I going to do about what happened, she was surprised when she knew that I didn't file a case against Kevin.

-Me-you can't be serious??

-Amber- yes I am, it was my fault, I brought this upon myself, I should have left him a long time ago but I thought I can change him if I put in some more time and effort, lucky for me Mrs.Artmn and Kelly noticed what I was trying to do, actually Mrs.Artmn apologized for Kevin's behavior and gave me this.

Then she reached under her pillow and pulled out a piece of paper and gave it to me, when I saw what it was my eye popped!!.

It was a huge check with enough money to start a new life anywhere.

-Amber-I can't blame other people for what I decide and I didn't want to take advantage of her, but when she knew that I'm not going to court she insisted that I accept the check.

-Me-wow!!, I think I got to get Kevin to beat me up too.

She laughed and said

-Amber-hey don't feel sorry for me ok, I'll be out of her in a week or so, just give me something to do I'm just bored of doing nothing these days, and I might need to crash at your place for a while after I get out of here, I'm leaving his sorry ass for good, I told Kelly that I will call her a day before I leave the hospital to get my stuff from Kevin's place.

-Me-ok cool but are you sure that you can use your hands no problems?

-Amber-come closer I'll prove it to you.

She tyred to grab my pants, I back up fast and laughed.

-Me-girl you're crazy, cool then I'll get you a lap top and send you the list of our sponsors and what we need to do coz we don't have much time with the amount of people getting into the fest this time.

-Amber-sure babe, just make sure you don't forget to buy me a new phone line to make the calls.

-Me-right, you got it Hun, just get some rest and I'll see you later today.

-Amber-ok come over her...

She hugged me, and then she kissed me & said.

-Amber- I never knew that there were chocolate Angeles on earth, but now I know there is at least one, honey I need you to hold on to this check for me until I get out ok.

-Me-are you sure, coz I might just skip town with it...

-Amber-no you won't, for two resons, number one is I trust you, number two is I know your mom.

-Me-ha ha you're one crazy white girl.

-Amber-you know I am Hun.

how can you not like this girl, she's just too sweet for her own good, I left the hospital and went to the nearest electronics shop, I bought a lap and a smart phone, by now it was almost lunch time, I called the guys at the shop and told them that I'll be back later so don't wait for me, then I drove straight home, for lunch and a nice nap.

I woke up to my phones message tone, well what you know, I got a message from ruby asking if I'm back in town, I replied yes, talk to you in a half an hour, after a quick wash I made myself a cup of coffee, went to my room and called ruby, I have to say it I'm starting to like how this girl calls me papi, she asked me if I can tune up her car to make it respond better to her driving style, I told her I can't promise but I'll see what I can do, coz it's a private time at the garage for me and my boys to work on their cars, she asked me if I was free later and I said maybe in a few hours, so she said she'll call me when she leaves work,I got dressed up and left home straight to the police station to get some paper work started for the permit to use an old abandoned air strip just outside of town just like every time, and also let them know that I need to go check out the place tomorrow morning so I won't get in any trouble.

when I was done with that I went to the hospital to give amber the stuff I got her, and show her what needed to be done, I got to the hospital, went to her room to find her in tears.

-Me-are you ok Hun, should I call the nurse or the doctor?

-Amber-no it's not that...

-Me-then what is it?

-Amber-Kevin was here half an hour ago, he came to make things right he said, apparently his mom gave him a hard time about what he did to me, and he wanted to apologize and make it up to me trying to open a new page and make things better, but he wasn't ready when I told him that I'm not coming back and I've had more than enough of him hurting me.....

-Me-I guess he didn't take it well...

-Amber-no he didn't, I think his anger started to take over, lucky for me the doctor came in to check on me, then he just went quiet and left, I got really scared DJ.

-Me-maybe I should go have a chat with him, to straighten things out.

-Amber-no...no please don't, I don't want you to get in trouble because of me, promise me you won't, DJ promise me please..

-Me-if that's what you want then fine, I'll let it go this time, but are you going to be ok?, you need a smoke or something (joking)!!.

-Amber-ooh I wish, don't worry about me Hun, I'll be fine, so what goodies have you got for me ??

I got the stuff out and we got started on work, we almost lost track of time but I had to leave coz it was time for ambers dinner and meds, she should get some rest,I made sure she was feeling better before I left, kissed her good night and told her that if she needs anything she can call me anytime, I passed by the garage to check that everything was locked and as I was just getting back in my car I got a call from ruby, she asked where I was, I told her that I'm about to leave the garage, she asked if we can have dinner together and she's paying for it, how can I refuse a free meal ?, I asked where at?, she said if I wait she'll buy it and come to the garage, I was cool with that actually coz I was hungry for some chicken pasta from a restaurant near her with some garlic bread so I went in the garage called home told mom that I'm eating out, there's something weird about a girl buying a man a meal, you can be almost 90% sure that she wants something from you.

half an hour later I got a message from ruby saying (I'm outside), I went downstairs and after a warm hug and a kiss I picked up the dinner bags and we went upstairs, I already had the table set and we sat down for a warm delicious meal, as we were chatting about what's going on I told her about what happened to amber and she said she wanted to come with me next time I go to the hospital,then we talked about her car and how she can get the best of its performance, she wanted to race in the fest this time, I told her it's not a beginners thing, she can lose money or worse her car, coz some racers bet pink slips or cash between them as they approach the starting line.

so this time it's better to be on the line and watch what goes down up close, I asked her if she would like to help by being on the organizing team and she loved it, needless to say we spent the night at the garage and I had my dessert, what can I say she missed her sugar papi, ruby gets to spend some time with me whenever Kevin leaves town, so some times Kevin is away for a few days and when the cat is away the mice will play, personally I don't care if Kevin knows about what's going on between ruby and I, doesn't bother me one bit, but for ruby it means more comfort, so he won't be around to ask questions and give her a hard time.

next morning I woke up got in the shower came out to the smell of fresh coffee a hot breakfast and a beautiful smiling face, she had some coffee while I put my clothes on and said that she had to leave to get a few things done and we might meet later tonight, as for me I had my meal and went down to open the garage for the guys to come in to finish some work on their cars and I went straight to the police station to get my permit, I had to wait for just a few minutes for it to be stamped.

while I was waiting I heard some of the police men talking about some people coming in to report more stolen cars, and that it has increased lately, but their biggest problem was that the cars are nowhere to be found, not even in the states around us, as if they vanished in thin air, I got really worried coz this can mess up the street king fest reputation, I might lose the whole thing, people might stop coming coz they don't want their cars stolen, it's that simple, I needed to make a few phone calls to get to the bottom of this.

my papers are done, I drove to the air strip to check it out and see if anything can be done to improve on it or needs to be fixed or maintained, it took a while for me to check out the place but I finally wrote my notes and shot a few videos and took some pictures of the place, now I got to hit the road back coz it was getting hot and I'm getting hungry, on my way back I called amber to see how she was doing and gave her some of the details of what needs to be done in the air strip, who to contact of our sponsors, I sent her the videos and pictures when I got to the garage, I'm happy to hear that amber is doing well and managing her time with helping me with sending a few e-mails or calling some of our sponsors, I think she likes it.

which gave me time to put my ears to the ground to find out what's really going on with the car thefts, I called a few guy in different crews who knew other guys who owned chop shops, I'm trying to find anyone who knows about the warehouse full of cars at the docks, but nobody knew about it period, so I knew that I had to see what was going on in that place myself.

these two weeks passed like lightning, with all the racers arriving to town and getting all of them into the race list, running around to get the air strip prepared, setting up sale booths, printing tickets and t-shirts, some of the racers stayed in hotels others had vans or campers others we had to set up living quarters for them with in the air strep, we made use of every inch of that place, but despite are best efforts some more cars still went missing, although we did our best to warn people about it but it happened, I heard that some of the cars had tracking systems and alarms on them but still the alarms didn't work and the tracking systems fail to show where the cars are, you know that this wasn't just petty theft work, and to keep the faith in our fest I refunded the entrance fee to the racers that reported their cars stolen.

ruby has been around for most of the time, she really helped with organizing a lot, through this she became a good friend to amber, they connected on some level maybe coz they hated the same guy when, we all sat worked and ate together, I spent some time with ruby to improve her skills on driving, took her to a few small races to see how well she does, I retuned her car, now we are just a few days away from the start of the fest.

we had an unfinished race with the guys near the docks remember, so I called Yoshi to tell him we need to finish this, we went there to meet them and there was Yoshi with a few of his boys and his younger sister Kim waiting, Kim is a an expert racer with a passion for new American muscle cars and drives a Camaro, Yoshi was the leader of the crew so he gets the final say on who races or not, so the racers were his pick for tonight, by now ruby knows the rules so she picked the car that she thought would go for a short race and she nailed it, she chose the Camaro, Kim's car and Kim chose a quarter mile race, ruby got very excited, but she managed to keep the poker face as best as she could.

short race, two girls, this should be interesting, I took ruby aside to give her some tips, I told her not to underestimate Kim, the girl knows how to handle her car, her car is well modified and both cars are almost with in the same power range, but I have faith in you and how how I tuned your car, Kim will mostly go for nitrous at the final stretch,but you need to do it a bit earlier this time, your car will shift gears in the mid yellow rpm, when you hit third gear go for the nitrous this will push you ahead, so when Kim hits her button she'll run out of distance to catch up with you, hopefully you'll finish in front, there's some money on the line in this race, win and you'll get some, lose and I'll spank that ass, she was on edge so I wanted to loosen her up with a little joke, she smiled and said then it's a win win for me, what can I say, she gets it, I felt her confidence in her skills, I meant her driving skills as she turned around and walked wagging her tail all the way back to her car.

the moment of truth has come, cars at the start line streets are clear ahead, engines are revving hard as the girls look into each other's eyes like two lionesses about to get into battle, the bet between me and Yoshi was 500 $ plus some spare parts that we owned and none of us wants to sell them to the other for a long time, if I win I get the parts that I want from him and if he wins he gets the parts that he wants from me, nothing to worry about just to give this race a bit of an edge to make things interesting between me and Yoshi, but for ruby this was the time to graduate and earn the name street racer for real, and racing someone like Kim is a real test, it's time to make it happen.

tension at its peak, as soon as the starter hit the light they jumped of the start line like rockets, Kim really showed skill in handling that car, a smooth start less tire burn than ruby but still ruby held her ground as they were very close off the start line with Kim just inches ahead, through first gear and still the same, second gear Kim was pulling ahead bit by bit crawling away, at the start of the third gear ruby went for the nitrous button and managed to rocket ahead by a car length, coz the boost lasted through the whole gear length.

Kim was caught by surprise when she saw ruby flying by and hit her nitrous at almost the end of third gear, when her gear shifted into forth the race was almost sealed, the nitrous boost stopped in the middle of forth gear which gave ruby the advantage of winning with a little more than a fender, which Kim couldn't believe, she thought she lost to a beginner, what she doesn't know is that it was a well planned strategy, ruby came back with that wild jungle cat look in her eyes, like she just caught her first pray, so proud of her self coz she earned it, lucky for her that I'm a good friend of Yoshi and Kim otherwise Kim would have ate her alive.

after everybody left the time was still early so we all went to have dinner at Yoshi's family restaurant which wasn't far from where we were, we spoke about the car thefts and how it was affecting the street fest over a nice hot meal, and how weird it was that none of Kevins crew reported a stolen car, me and Yoshi stepped aside and I asked Yoshi if he knew anything about the warehouse at the docks that I saw when I was chased the last time we raced here.

but Yoshi didn't know anything about it, he was really surprised when I told him about it, then I asked him about what he thinks if we went there for a sneak peek and he was all for it, we needed to be very quiet about it, so I told ruby to wait with Kim coz I'm going with Yoshi to get the parts he owes me we won't take long.

we left the restaurant from the back door, and coz we had to be quiet we drove there in one the delivery cars, Yoshi knew the docks better than I did, he told me that this side of the dock was declared off limits for civilians by the ports management a couple of years ago, since then the place was dark and empty, we parked our car at a safe distance away from the warehouse in a dark corner.

we stud out there just listening for any noise in the wend, we can hear the waves crashing against the shipping docks, we can hear the street behind the port but there was no sound of machinery, the place was really quiet, just when we wanted to move towards the warehouse we heard sound of a car approaching the place, we stayed back in our corner and saw a car going towards the warehouse and stopped in front of it, then the door opened slowly and we heard the sound of the machines inside, the light hit the car when the door was fully opened to my surprise it was Kevin's black corvette.

the place was sound proofed so well that you can't hear whatever that's going on inside almost a few meters away from it, it's like they built a warehouse inside the warehouse, the car went inside, the door closed and suddenly the noise stopped, as if nothing was there, we moved closer trying to find a way to look inside but there was no windows to be found, we found metal stairs on the far side of the warehouse, so we climbed to the roof to try to find an air vent or something, but the ones that we found were isolated for sound proofing so we couldn't hear or see anything.

we were about to leave when Yoshi stumbled on an old trap door, we opened it and there was a ladder leading down to a bridge on top of the roof of the sound proofed work shop under us, I think this bridge is used to maintain the air ducts, we walked very carefully on the bridge untill we found somewhere we can see clearly from, we stayed there for a few minutes to check out what was going on in there, I recognized a few of the cars that were being taken to pieces and saw Kevin talking to some of the workers pointing out to them what to do with some parts.

then he went to a corner that had a table with some sort of electronic device on it that was linked to a muscle car next to it, I was surprised to see the whiz kid Bruce change there, I think it was way passed his bed time but they might be testing something on that muscle car, it was very clear that Kevin ran the place and that device really made me curious coz it didn't look like any engine upgrade I know, Itook out my phone and shot a few videos of Kevin and the place but it wasn't very clear, Yoshi suggested we get a bit closer but it wasn't that easy, as we looked around we found a ladder but it wouldn't be a very good idea at the time, coz it would put us in a place very close to the workers, and that meant getting caught very easy, so we left that plan aside for another time.

time to get out of this place and get back to the girls at the restaurant, coz we almost spent an hour on this spy mission, climbing out of that trap door wasn't as easy as getting in it but we finally made it out, we got to the car and a few minutes later we got to Yoshi's place to get the parts he owed me, I collected my winnings and went back to the restaurant.

when we got there the place was closing down, only ruby and Kim were there, I got in the car with ruby, and as she was driving me back home she told me that Amber called her, and she said the doctor told her that she can leave the hospital tomorrow if she wants too, that meant she'll be crashing at the garage which made me think what's Kevin going to do about it if he knew about it.

to say the truth it was a risk I would gladly take for Amber, we got to the garage, I took the parts inside and went upstairs to chill out a bit, coz tonight was a special night for Ruby, she felt like she finally became a street racer, that's when she caught me by surprise when she unleashed her inner wild cat on me, she even had leopard print underwear on, it was a rumble in the jungle night, man ooh man what a night.

next morning after Ruby left I had to check out what's going on at the air strip, and after that I had to pass by the hospital to pick up amber on my way back, so I had my cup of coffee and made myself a snack for the road then I went down stairs and unlocked the garage for the my boys to finish working on their cars and I hit the road, I got to say this street fest felt different it was bigger than usual, more racers and more sponsors than we ever had before.

when I got to the place it looked amazing, everything was according to plan, some guys were almost done testing start lights and cameras, the speakers and sound systems working great, the race track was redone from start to finish, the stands from the start to the end were ready, all we have to do is just start racing, I was so excited I couldn't stop smiling all the time I was there, I couldn't believe that I was responsible for all of this, I called amber to see if she was getting ready to leave the hospital,and she said she will be ready by the time I get there.

half an hour later I was at the hospital to pick her up, she was waiting in the lobby when I got there, I just parked outside picked up her bag, and helped her into the car and got out of there, it was lunch time so I asked amber what would she like for lunch, lucky for me she was in the mood for Chinese, I took the nearest left turn to reach our destination.

suddenly I heard cars hitting the brakes hard after I turned, I looked in my rear view mirror and saw another car turned behind us, I knew we were being followed by, I asked amber if anyone else knows about her leaving the hospital today, she said she called Kelly yesterday and asked her to get her stuff from Kevin's place and keep them with her untill she calls her later to pick them up, well I guess that solves the mystery of who's following us, I didn't tell amber that we were followed coz I didn't want her to get stressed out.

I asked her if it was ok if we have lunch at the restaurant coz I was too hungry to wait untill we get back to the garage and she was ok with it, we went inside got a table, ordered our food and as we were waiting I told amber that I was going to the pharmacy next to the restaurant for a few minutes, on my way out I described the car that was following us to the waiter and told him they were friends of mine, and asked him to go and see what would the like to have for a takeout lunch and add it to my bill, then I went to the pharmacy got a few things for myself plus two bottles of their best fast acting laxative.

I paid the man went back to the restaurant to find our food was already on the table, and the take out order was ready too, so I went near the kitchen counter, asked the waiter to bring out the order, I added the laxative to all the stuff they ordered then asked him to take it out to them, when I got back to the table I just couldn't hide the smile on my face, Amber noticed that I was up to no good and said ..
-Amber-I know that smile on your face, come on tell me what di you do ?.
I giggled and said...
-Me-don't worry about it, let's just finish our meal and get you back the garage so you can get some rest.

after about 45 minutes we were almost done with our after meal and the laxative has taken its effect on the guys out side, coz they came storming into the resturant screaming trying hold themselves as best as they can racing towards the toilet at the back of the restaurant, it was a small restaurant and the toilet had one stall in it, so it's either they shared it or one of them used the sink, when Amber saw them she knew who they were and she laughed out loud like a little girl then she looked at me and said….
-Amber-so that's what you been up to!.
I was in tears coz of laughing so hard, I told her…
-Me-that's what they get for following us, I wasn't about to let roll by that easy.
I paid for our food and left the restaurant back to the garage coz I really needed to take a nap after this, and I was really glad to see amber smiling like that again, and the guys that followed us well I don't know what time they left the restaurant, but I gave the waiter some money to buy them old folks diapers from the pharmacy next door so he can get them out of the toilet.

We were laughing all the way back to the workshop, Amber called Kelly to bring her stuff to the workshop, minutes after we got there Kelly arrived I took the bags upstairs and Kelly helped her unpack some of her clothes, I didn't have that much space at the chill space in the workshop and you know how much clothes women have, they got the basics out but the rest of the clothes stayed the bags until I buy another closet or two maybe, basically the next few of days were devoted to Amber and getting her comfortably settled in, all preparations for the fest are done we are ready to get it started.

later that night I woke up to a weird surprise, the Kevin kind, yep amber calls me up to tell me that Kevin is at the garage with a couple of his boys, I told amber that I'll be there as fast as I can, I got there as quickly as humanly possible, Kevin was still there, he looked a bit out of control, I couldn't figure out if he was high or drunk out of his damn mind, I parked my car and walked up to him calmly and said..
-Me-hey Kevin….you know this is trespassing right?
one of his boys stepped to me and said it's none of your damn business, Kevin actually turned around, smacked him upside the head and said..
-Kevin- we are on his property you dump ass!

I almost busted out laughing but I had to keep a straight face, then Kevin looked at me and said ..

-Kevin- I know you have amber in there, I want my girl back and I won't leave without her.

-Me-Kevin I know that you're smart enough to know that she won't go back with you after what you done to her, what happened Kev, Tina is no fun anymore?

-Kevin-that gold digging junky, you know after her boyfriend got busted she threw herself in my arms crying, I was actually trying to be nice to her and help her out of her sadness over losing him, all she did was mess up my life with cocaine and other stuff and stuck to me like glue where ever I go, she was a dependent junky, dragged me into it just so she can feed on whatever I get, she has a problem with almost every one of my crew, the guys and their girls, I kicked her ass out days ago and I had some time to think about what I did to amber,I was wrong to treat Amber the way I did ...

-Me-Kevin this not couples therapy, it's good to know that you have finally knew your mistake, but it's too late now, you're lucky that Amber is not taking you to court for what you did to her and asked me not to do anything to you .

-Kevin-ooh yea ... you think that am afraid of you?

then he pulls a gun to my face, for a few seconds I stared him dead in his eyes, it was one of those crazy moments, then I pulled a Jackie Chan on him and took the gun from his hand and pointed it to his chest, if you remember the movie rush hour Jackie Chan and Chris tucker in the street scene when Jackie pulled the gun from Chris tuckers hand with fast twist, you will know what I mean, I couldn't believe that I did it, but still I had to keep my game face on, Kevin was stunned, mouth open and eyes gazing at me, he couldn't believe what just went down, I think at that moment in time his buzz was gone, I kept staring at him with a mad look in my eyes, and I told him

-Me-I could have put you in the same hospital in a bed next to her room the same day Kevin bt lucky for you I was out of town at the time, you know that Amber and I go way back, I'm the closest thing to family she's got in this town, Amber didn't want any trouble, she didn't even want to take you to court for what you did, how could you do this to her, she was your sisters friend even your mom likes her, what the hell were you thinking when you did that to her?

then one of his boys pulls out a gun and points it at me, when I saw that I slowly started to slide the gun down Kevin's chest all the way until I got it between his tummy and his pants pointing down as I was looking at his boy, I told him
-Me- if you shoot me I might shot Kevin's dick off and then he'll kill you or do the same shit to you and both of you might live like bitches for the rest of your miserable lives
so he put his gun back in his pants, suddenly I felt a sneeze coming on, I tried to hold it back but I couldn't, I sneezed and pulled the trigger and the gun went off, it was a scary moment for all of us, time stod still as the sound of the shot echoed around us, thank god the bullet missed Kevin and went in the grass between Kevin's feet.
I can guaranty that Kevin became 100% sober after that incident, I looked down to see what happened and there was no blood, I was surprised that Kevin didn't wet himself so I smiled and looked up at his face to see the shock expression on his face, his eyes were wide open, lips shivering and he wasn't breathing, I had to bring him out of it, so I said dude I didn't mean to do that but no worries your junk is still intact, he finally exhaled .

I got worried coz I though he was going to turn into angry smurf coz he was starting to turn blue with some sweat on the side of his face, and I think I saw I single tear roll down his left eye, good thing he was wearing low waist baggie jeans, all this happened while amber was watching from a window up top, she saw it all from the beginning untill the end.

A nearby police car must have heard the gun shot, coz in less than a minute there was a flash light shining on us and a policeman asking...
-Policeman-what's going on here?
Then he got out of the police car and walked into the garage yard coming towards us, I quickly but the gun in the back of my jeans and pulled my jacket down.
-Policeman-good evening gentlemen, do you mind telling me what you are doing here at this time of night?
-Me-oh nothing much sir this is my old friend Kevin and this is my workshop, as you maybe know about the street king fest is around the

corner, so he came around to see if I can do a lastminute upgrade on his car that's all sir.

-Policeman-I see, we heard a gunshot coming from around here, do you gentlemen know anything about that?

-Me- yea we head it too, sounded like it came from the other side of the street, but coz of the buildings I can't really be sure where from exactly sir. I can tell that the officer didn't buy my story coz he had that I don't believe you look in his eyes, he didn't notice the hole in the grass where the bullet went coz Kevin smartly covered it by stepping on it, the policeman turned to Kevin and took a good look at him then asked him...

-Policeman-you're Kevin Artmn is that correct?

-Kevin-yes sir.

-Policeman-I heard that your dad is running for mayor, you better not be causing any trouble son.

-Kevin-no sir, I wouldn't dream of it, and I really hope that I can count on your support for my dad.

-policeman- Mr.Artmn is a good man, me and the boys back at the station wish him luck and he can count on our votes, you can be sure of that, you boys have a good night and stay out of trouble you hear ?.

He said that as he walked back to the police car, we smiled and thanked him for his concern for keeping the peace on the streets, I turned to Kevin and said...

-Me-so dad wants to be mayor ha??

-Kevin-what's it to you?

-Me-I'm just worried that it's going to make you a bigger dick then what you already are Kev.

ooh I tipped him off and now he is reaching behind his back looking for his gun, but it wasn't there, I pulled it out from the back of my jeans and said

-Me-it's here bro, wow man your short term memory sucks, better cut down on that shit you're stuffing up your nose, coz it's really starting to show on you, look man let's leave it here, let Amber be, take your boys and go home and if she wants you she'll come back you know it and I know it .

he took a long look at me before he turned his back and left, he didn't say a word but I felt it inside me that this won't be over any time soon, I got back in my car and as I was driving back home it accrued to me to call my friend Jeff in L.A, I asked him to get me in contact with the party photographer asap, he said he'll have him call me soon, I parked my car at home I called

Amber to see if she was ok and tell her to be careful coz I felt that Kevin won't let her go or what happened tonight that easy, after that I went back to bed to end a very eventful day.

next morning I took Amber out for breakfast, then the bank so she can deposit the check that Kevin's mom gave her in her account, after that I showed her some of what she helped to put together for the fest, then went shopping for some furniture, the photographer called me while we were shopping, turns out he's a real cool guy, I asked him for whatever pictures from the birthday party that shows Mr.Artmn and his candy girl together asap, he said he'll hook me up as soon as he can get them ready and for a bit extra he will throw in the negatives, it sounded like a sweet deal to me so I took it .

we met with Ruby for lunch and some Italian gelato after that, then later we went back to the workshop, and to end a great day for Amber Ruby suggested we hit the movies so we did that after sunset, after that we took dinner back to the garage coz amber had to take her night medication and get some rest, as we all should coz next morning all that we worked for in the past weeks comes to reality.

finally the day has come and here we are at the official street king fest opening, it was nothing short of a carnival, we had the racers and sponsors parade, the DJ is playing the hottest tracks, we had huge balloons all around the place, then the introduction of our sponsors and racers so everybody gets to know everybody, after that as the sun was setting some of our local dance crews showed some of their skills on the dance floor, the BBQ pits were blazing, cold drinks all around for the kids and adults, there was something for everyone, needless to say me and my crew were making sure that things are running smoothly.

the party went on untill night fall, after that everyone had to get some rest coz the next day is the start of the real deal, the day went great with some minor incidents but nothing serious, but the result was a great start of a new era for the street king fest, I felt that my velvet dream was coming true, I'm stepping into my new diamond life style, a life of luxury and wealth, as I laid down on my bed after having a small celebration dinner with amber and ruby, the night would have been perfect if I could have spent the night with the girls but I went home instead coz I had I big day coming, and ruby stayed with amber at the garage for protection.

morning time, a cool easy breezy weather, the races will start shortly just as soon as the racers lottery ends, each racer has a number, numbers are picked at random, no categories followed, we don't Mach engine size or power, cars line up according to the numbers picked in the lottery, so when it's your time you better bring it all to the table, I've seen crazy miracles happen in these races, engine failures, miss starts, crashes, you name it anything can happen,you gotta have nerves of steel, ice water in your veins and brass balls to make it here, I saw people freeze on the start line, top dogs went down and under dogs went to the top, you can call it a game of luck or skill or whatever you want to call it, this is the street king fest, welcome to the big boys league.
every day the lottery runs in the morning and by the end of the day many racers fall out, simple and basic losers leave and winners stay to fight another day, and Ruby keeps getting hotter and hotter every day, she keeps smiling, winking, dropping hints, stealing kisses like teenagers sometimes or dirty looks whenever we come close, but someone has started to notice all that, yea you guessed it Kevin, I can really see that he had his doubts about me and Ruby are becoming a reality, plus the fact that Amber left him and is staying with me is not putting a smile on his face.

It's strange enough that Kevin have lasted this long, I know he has some skills but not enough to reach where he is now he hasn't lost a race yet and climbing up the list like a rocket,It seems that he wasn't kidding when he said he had something special for his first time in street fest, I think he wants to make a huge impression on every one, an undefeatable fresh face, he goes into every race looking so damn confidant that he's going to win like he knows it and sure enough he does, there's one other strange thing, I heard some people complaining about their cameras or some devices not working well at certain times.

these people were viewers that sat at both sides of the track, and after talking to some of them they said the same thing it happens when Kevin races his car, even some of the professional camera crews that were filming the races had the same complaints and pointed out the same car, especially the ones at the middle and the end of the track, something had to be done.

so I spoke to some of the guys that lost to Kevin, I asked them about what do they think went wrong and caused them to lose the race, all of them spoke of electric or electronic problems, sometimes their cars just act weird for a few seconds just enough for Kevin to catch up or pass them, some of them checked their cars after the race and found burned car computer or fuses, some said the car gauges just went nuts for a few seconds and went back to normal after that, but this happened to them when they raced Kevin only .

after consulting with the technical judges we came to a conclusion that someone was using an EMP gun but we couldn't know where this person might be, so thanks to one of our sponsors we set up scots with electrical gauges around the race track the next day, just to see where the signal would be strongest so we can pin point the source, we had to put an end to this coz the next couple of days are the real deal, the finals are upon us.

here we are at crunch time of the street king fest, usually it's three days long but this time we had so many racers it went to five days of tire burning, engine revving and pushing cars and drivers to their absolute limits events, two number drawings a day one in the morning and another after 6 pm, winners race twice today, so we might have a bigger chance of finding the where the EMP is hidden, the heat is on and drivers are on their toes.

coz tomorrow is the last day, only 12 drivers will race for the number 1 spot and it's going to be at night, one way or the other we have to find the EMP, we are left with about 48 races with two events today we should end up with 12 for tomorrow, the day went smoothly, Kevin won twice, the EMP signal was noticed almost at half the race track towards the finish, but nobody saw anyone holding a gun or a device during Kevin's races.

I thought might be hidden in one of the viewers camera or something like that, then I remembered when Kevin said that he had a special car and what I saw at Kevin's warehouse at the docks,that car he is driving now was hooked to some device that looks like no car part I know, my guess is that The EMP is actually installed on the car, my last chance to find out is tomorrow but how, can't just walk up to Kevin and ask him to open the hood, so it's tomorrow or never, ooh lady luck where are you now...

I had a couple of almost sleepless nights coz of this, I'm burning brain cells trying to find a way to check Kevin's car but no luck so far, today is the last day, no morning racing today, so I spent my morning at the garage with the girls brain storming on how to expose Kevin, but still no ideas, the good thing that happened this morning is that I got a delivery from L.A, the pictures finally arrived, so I asked amber to keep them safe for me, then I left to the bus station & put the negatives in a small locker then straight back home and gave the key to my mom for safe keeping, I had my lunch then went up to my room, had a spliff to help me chill my mind after that I had a nap after setting the timer to wake me at 6 pm, coz I have to be at the track a bit early today.

I woke up to find a few missed calls on my phone from Ruby and a member of the judging comity, I called ruby back and she told me that there might be a small problem with today's races, some of the racers are refusing to race unless we do something about Kevin, so I said ok I'll be there asap,I washed up and fixed myself a snack and got in my car, I called the judge to see if I can get more details, the man told me it seems like the racers have been talking about what happened to the ones who raced Kevin and the damage that came to their cars after racing with him .

they demand to check his car for technical safety reasons, personally I wouldn't blame them, some of these guys have spent crazy amounts of cash on their cars and wouldn't want to risk any damage if they can help it, looks like lady luck has been doing her job after all, I asked the judge to round up the racers, I hanged up and put my foot on the gas hard to try to get there asap to get this issue resolved before race time.

by the time I got there everybody was there except Kevin, the racers said that they will not race unless we find a solution for this problem, that would devastate the finals and the fest all together, at this time Kevin arrived to the scene and said that he just been told about this emergency meeting, I had to give to him as it was, he didn't like it at first and said that there is no regulation to back up the racers claim and he was right, but there is a first time for everything .

I told him if it was one or two even if five of them wanted this we might dismiss their complaint, but all of them are on it, that would mean canceling all the races today and we simply can't do that, one thing about Kevin is sometimes he doesn't know when to fold his cards, so he decided to let the technical judges check his car, now we are about an hour or a bit more away from starting the racers drawing for who's racing who for the final night.

the judges went through the car inch by inch, they almost gave up on finding anything untill one of them noticed that the crank shaft had an extra pulley that had a belt that turns a secondary alternator located almost under the engine, it was well hidden, they followed the wire links from that to a secondary battery inside the car in a customized space in the glove compartment, then the wires ran under the car to the front bumper where the device was hidden, it was linked to the nitrous bottom, so nitrous and EMP run together at the same time, when Kevin was informed of the result he denied knowing anything about that, and said that his mechanic promised him an unbeatable car and that's it .

I knew he was lying but the judges decided to give him a choice either he removes the EMP or get kicked out of the race, I took Kevin a few steps away from the judges and told him
-Me- if you retire from the races now I'll ask the judges not to announce this result, it will look like you had enough and left the fest without losing a single race which will be really good for you, come on Kev you know that you don't need the prize money, leave it for someone else.
-Kevin-did you put them up to this ?.
-Me-no man I swear it wasn't my idea, but because you used the EMP in almost every race you exposed yourself, you only have yourself to blame for this.
he finally decided to retire from the fest with a look in his eyes that told me that he didn't believe that I had nothing to do with it, and it's not over yet, which added one more scar to the rivalry between us.

thank god we finished the fest without problems, we had to bring up one more racer into the top 12, so we chose the racer with the best time to complete the set and got it done, tonight was amazing, the last races were breath taking and very close at the finish line, people got the full flavor of the street king fest, the king was crowned at the end in a huge celebration with lots of tire smoke, loud music and fireworks, the fest ended in a carnival as big as it started, it was a night to remember, me and the girls were standing high in the judges both looking over the whole thing, just soaking in all that's going on in front of us, it was amazing .

we had a blast in making alloff this come together, it was the biggest fest yet, for me it was the closest feeling to knowing that the woman you love gave birth to a beautiful healthy baby, I was almost in tears of joy but I had to hide it from the girls, we just stood there holding hands just watching what's going on until the end of it all, we had our celebration and now it's time to go home, I drove the girls back to the workshop, ruby took her car and left and amber went in and I went home for a good night sleep.

next morning I got a call from amber, saying that the police are here and asking for you, I was surprised to hear that, but I had to go see what's the reason for this early visit, I got my clothes on and a few minutes later I got to the workshop to find police cars surrounding the place, I saw amber and asked her if she knew anything about this and she said no, but they're waiting for you upstairs, we went upstairs to find super cop jake and a detective having coffee as they were waiting for me..

-Me-good morning gentlemen, by all means make your selves at home.
-Jake- you finally showed up.
-Detective-good morning Mr. Jackson
-Me-how can I be of assistance to our towns finest?
-Jake-you're getting sloppy DJ.
-Me-what is he talking about detective?
-Detective-we received an anonymous tip about where to find some of the recently stolen cars.
-Me-and what does that have to do with me?
-Detective-it says the cars are at your shop and you've been using some of them as parts to upgrade other customers cars or sell them as used spare parts.
-Me-no sir I do not know or do any of that, we only use brand new parts to be sure that we do a great job, I buy my parts from the shops around town, I'm a good costumer at almost all of them you can ask them yourself,pulse I keep all the receipts and a file of every car that came to my workshop.

I turned around at Jake and saw a strange look in his eyes with a crocked smile, it was like he knew something I didn't know.

-Detective-we waited for you to come in so we can take a look around your place if you don't mind
-Me- its ok, feel free to check the place.

they went around uncovering the few cars in the garage, checking numbers until they got to the back door of the garage, the detective asked me about what's behind that door and I said this where we take out the trash, he opened the door went out and just saw the big trash container, this is where Jake jumped in and said look behind the container detective, I felt a sudden chill down my spine, then I walked with the detective around the container and saw 3 almost disassembled half covered cars parked behind it, one of them was Shawn's car the green lantern, I was shocked, the detective looked at me and said ….
-Detective-do you have any knowledge about these cars Mr. Jackson?
-Me-I know the owner of the green car, he's a friend of mine, I helped him build it, he came to see me the next day it was stolen weeks ago, but I don't know anything about the other cars, and I don't keep cars in this place ever.

they checked the chassis numbers on the cars and they Mached some of the numbers of the stolen cars in the list they had, I knew who did this to me but I had no way of proving it, the images and videos on my phone of Kevin's chop shop won't be that good coz they were not very clear, so explaining all that to the detective won't do me any good, right now I'm facing theft charges for god knows how many cars and if they can stick that to me it means a long time in jail, should I run or let the law take its course, I knew one thing for sure I need a good lawyer asap, it seems that Kevin was really on fire, he didn't let it go that easy, but I didn't expect it to be this fast !!.

Jake put the handcuffs on me even before the detective started reading my rights, as we were leaving the workshop I looked up to amber and told her to find me a lawyer, to keep a long story short Kevin's father used his friends the chief of police and court judges to get this done quicly, even at my court hearing my lawyer had an accident on his way to court and ended up in the hospital and I was rushed to jail.

first week was very hard, I was just trying to adjust and fit in, it wasn't easy, but day by day I started meeting guys that were street racers that ended up here because of Kevin or Kevin's dad or both, they offered them jobs getting illegal drugs across state lines or stashing them in their house for a short while with the promise of paying them in full after the job is done, and then some of them got caught,then they get another deal that if they keep their mouth shut the money will go to their family, and they will be taken good care of until the guy gets out of jail .

they told me about the way they get the shipments from California to NY is through events like car shows or races, and there is always some event going on in a states along the way to NY, they carry some in race cars or spare parts trailers, and within the events drugs and cash get exchanged in tool boxes or a whole trailer or a car gets a new owner, or sometimes big amounts get cut down to smaller portions and some are stashed in racing cars or show cars, and Kevin sometimes gets to supervise these transactions, coz not all the amount goes to NY, some of it is sold along the way to buyers in states on the travel route, while Mr.Artmn makes his calls to ensure safe crossings through state lines.

Now I know how Mr.Artmn was helping to clean the city streets!, I knew some of these guys, they make a living out of racing and car shows, some of them have no other income to support their family's so they have to do what they are told in this case, god knows if Mr.Artmn kept his word to them or not but it is what it is for now, some of these guys are spending a few years here, the drivers some time get paid in cash or get the money in their bank accounts, some of them are registered as employees for Kevin or Mr.Artmn, and when they get caught Kevin and Mr.artmn say they have no knowledge about the drugs .

one weird thing happened in jail, I kept seeing this one prisoner that nobody seems to know anything about, some even say they don't recall seeing that person I'm describing to them,at times when he's there he keeps monitoring me from a distance, I pointed him out to some of the guys but I got the same answer never saw him before now or he must be new, he disappears for days then shows up for a day or two max, he was about around 6 feet tallhe bald big man dark skin looks like a football player, always wears black shades, even the guards don't remember seeing him with the inmates, I walked towards him one time when I saw him standing in the shade in the jail yard, he just turned around and walked away slowly like he was going back to his cell, I followed him but he just disappeared in the crowd, simply vanished like a ghost, the thought of this guy might be a hit man contracted to kill me kept me on edge, he certainly looked like one.

I got a few visits from my family and some friends, Amber came by one day and she looked really scared, she told me that Kevin came by the workshop last night he was drunk and screaming, he asked her to go back with him to his place, he told her that he wants her back or else, his exact words were (if I can't have you no one else will), I told her to leave the place and go stay with Ruby for a while until things cool down, it's safer for her to be with ruby for now, after all no one know what Kevin might do next, the last thing this guy needs is emotional stress, it can burn out his last fuse, meaning that he can snap in an instant and do something really stupid, god I wish I was out there, now am getting worried about my family, Amber and my workshop.

a few days later a little after midnight two of the night shift guards came to my cell and called and me out, when I asked why they told me that someone is here to see me, the first thing that came to my mind was that Kevin or his dad had paid someone to harm me in some way, they took me to an office and asked me to wait inside and left.

this room had no windows, just a table with a few chairs and an air vent in the ceiling and that's it, oh and I think the door was sound proof too, perfect room for some of the crazy things that went through my mind at that time, then the door opened and Ruby walked in and closed the door behind her, she was like a breath of fresh air, when I looked at her I saw a badge on her waist, then I said out loud
-Me-I knew there was something different about you....
-Ruby-what do you mean??
-Me-you were just too clean to be a street girl.
-Ruby-oh come on, I wasn't that obvious
-Me-not only that but I built your car's engine when Carlos had it, my workshops logo was still on it, he was chased by the police and wrecked his car's rear end and got caught and he is in jail until now, someone took the engine out and the chassis number and built your purple Camaro and didn't change the name on the pink slip for some reason, I can't believe that Kevin didn't check up on you!.
-Ruby-I was just lucky I guess.

She hugged me and kissed me then said.

-Ruby-god knows how much I missed you papi, I'm really sorry that I didn't come to see you any time sooner, coz after you got caught Amber told me what happened and I was trying to find a way to help you get out of here, I finally was able to convince my superiors to get you out and that someone has framed you, then I told them that matters were getting worse with the car thefts and drugs distribution in your area

-Me-it's ok I understand, but are you sure that no one is watching us here?

-Ruby-don't worry this room is used by the FBI, no cams and no mics in here

-Me-so you are an F.B.I agent. !!

-Ruby-yes papi, agent Gabriella Sanchez F.B.I, corruption investigation division, we were investigating a case in your state when we came across George Artmn's name, Mr.artmn is working his way to the top to become mayor and has high hopes of reaching the senate and who knows what's next for him, his income was under investigation for some time, coz the amount he spends doesn't calculate with his income from managing his wife's businesses, the parties and the bribes were just over his budget limit, so we had to move in .

then Kevin's name came up shortly after, and after interrogating some of the racers that were caught they all said the same thing, what they were carrying belonged to someone they can't tell us about, coz they feared for their families wellbeing, a driver you knew who moved from NY to L.A after Kevin made a deal with him to be the link between Mexico and California, Carlos the previous owner of the engine u found in my car, he was in charge of getting drivers to smuggle the drugs from Mexico into the states, coz he knew some dirt rods in the desert to by pass the border security.

Carlos told us about you, he told us that you might be the only one who wouldn't be afraid of Kevin or his dad and would be willing to help if we can approach you without raising suspicions, we believe that Mr.artmn is involved in illegal drugs trafficking, bribery and corruption, and Kevin in illegal drugs trafficking and selling plus automotive theft, but why didn't you say anything when you found out about the car?

-Me-I had my doubts, I thought Kevin had a hand in this, so I waited to see what comes up later.

-Ruby-but this is not the only thing I came here for, I'm afraid I have some bad news...

when she said those words, pictures started going through my mind, I felt my heart skip a beat, I didn't say a word just waited for her to tell me what it was, praying to god in my heart that it didn't have anything to do with my family ...after a moment of silence she said..

-Ruby-the workshop caught fire last night and burned to the ground, Amber was in there when the fire broke out, she was the one who called 911 and she called me too, she escaped with minor injuries, and she managed to grab the security cams saving drive with her, Amber gave the drive to me, she couldn't talk much coz of inhaling a little bit too much smoke from the fire as she was getting out, she's in the hospital now, the doctors say she'll be ok they just need to keep her there for a few more days, most if not all of your equipments are gone, nothing could have saved the cars that were in there, drugs has reached a new level, school kids are getting access to cocaine and other stuff, it's like Kevin has been waiting for you to get out of the picture.

as she was telling me all this she also had pictures of the garage that she was showing me too, as I was looking at them images passed through my mind about the beautiful days I had in that place with my dad and my friends, I loved that place it was like a second home for me, the pictures showed a lot of damage but thank god that area near the exit gate at the back didn't suffer much fire damage, my eyes were burning as I fought the tears from falling, but I couldn't help it as a tear dropped on the pictures when I was looking at them .

my anger took over me coz of the pain that I felt at that moment, it's like someone has pinched my heart with pliers, when ruby saw the tear drop she asked if was ok, when I looked up at her she understood what I was going through at that time, she held my head to her chest and said you're leaving here with me tonight papi, we'll go to my headquarters and view the security cameras drive to see if it has anything useful and we'll take it from there, don't worry papi we'll get through this together.

I was about to explode until she told me that I'm getting out tonight, then someone knocked on the door, she opened the door and the person on the other side told her that they are ready and brought in some clothes, then she told me that she has one more detail to take care of and she'll be back in a few minutes to give me some time to change from the prison clothes, by the time she came back I was ready to leave this place, 5 minutes later I was in the back seat of a black SUV heading back to the city .

on are way she told that they have put a sleeper in my place, another prisoner was transferred from another prison to this prison and he almost looks like me, they brought him in wearing normal clothes as an FBI agent and now he's wearing my old prison clothes and I'm wearing the clothes he came in with, and they took him straight to solitary so this whole thing is on the down low so no word would reach Mr.Artmn or Kevin, according to prison records I'm still in jail..

on our way back we passed by the hospital to see amber, I went in alone, they put her in a private room, I had to make sure she was ok like ruby told me and thank god she was, I spoke to one of the nightshift doctors and he told me that she's fine, she can leave the hospital in a few days, that was a relief, it breaks my heart to see her that way, so I'm hoping that this will be the last time something bad happiness to her, I have to put an end to this, I just had enough of seeing that girl getting hurt by Kevin, he's going to pay for this in the worst way possible .

I went outside got in the SUV with ruby and we went to their secret headquarters, there we started planning on how to bring down Kevin and his dad, I told them about everything I know as well and what I learned in jail, I told them about the pictures I had of Mr.Artmn that I gave to amber for safe keeping which I think got lost in the fire, thank god I got the negatives hidden somewhere else, coz with these picture we can stop Mr.Artmn from using his influence to help Kevin, coz if these pictures get to Mrs. Artmn's hands it could be the end of him .

Whatever Mr.artmn owns is in her name, but he was spending what Kevin brings in from the drugs and stealing cars on the bribes and lavish parties and so on, so he lives on what he makes from managing what Mrs.Artmn owns from what her father left her, these pictures should put him between a rock and a hard place, it was almost dawn, so I had to get some sleep, I asked ruby to take me home. I called my little brother on the way back, and asked him to wait for me to let me in the house quietly.

by now just being in the house in my room having a shower and sleeping in my bed is just unbelievable, next morning my mom almost fainted and dad almost spit the coffee out of his mouth when I came down stairs for breakfast, they were happy to see me but worried about how I got out, I explained everything to them, I told them just to act normal like nothing has changed no one needs to know that I'm out or what am about to do.

I got the key from my mom but I didn't leave the house until nightfall, ruby picked me up, we went by the workshop I had to see it for myself, when we got there I was shocked, more than two thirds of the place is gone, by the time the firemen got there they managed to put the fire out before it burned the whole place down, my car was in there, but I know it had survived the flames coz it was parked at the exit gate of the workshop, in the part that didn't get much damage parked underground .

see not many of my friend know that I had a hydraulic car lift installed in that area underground keeping the car out of sight, now I just need a power source to get it working and get my baby out, I called jimmy, a friend of mine an electrician and a racer, I asked for his help and he was more than happy to help, and that he will be there in a bit over an hour, so I asked him to call me when he gets to the workshop or what's left of it, that gave us enough time to go get the negatives and maybe pass by the hospital to see Amber.

we got the negatives and got the pictures developed then went to see amber at the hospital, she was awake so we spent some time with her, then I got the call from my friend,he told me that he was on his way to the workshop, we left the hospital and got to the workshop and my friend has got everything almost ready, I kept my fingers crossed that my baby is ok, he connected the generator to what was left of the wires he found, then he flipped a switch and magic happened .

like a phoenix it rises from the ashes, my heart was beating like an African drum coz I was so happy that my baby was ok, only god knows how much time blood and sweat not to mention cash I had invested in this car, I started it and got it loaded on the shops trailer, I covered it and got it hooked to the SUV that Ruby came in, and wrapped everything up and thanked jimmy for his help and drove away with Ruby, I took the car to the secret headquarters to hide it there and work on our plan.

The F.B.I wants to catch Kevin red handed, I had to make that happen, I told them about the warehouse at the port, there has to be a storage warehouse very close to it, Ruby spent all her time at the shop and didn't know anything about Kevin's other operations, the guy is too deep when it came to hiding things, our best plan was to bust Kevin at the warehouse to make everything stick to him, and to make that happen they installed cameras around the place to see what's going on first.

during the next few days we learned a lot about Kevin's operation, his workers come to work and leave in a boat, and they come to work just after sun down and leave at dawn, they live on the other side of the port, some of the ports tug boats carry boxes of scrap metal and used parts back and forth from the warehouse to certain container ships in the port, I got to say Kevin runs a tight operation, with a storage area right next door he was well set, now all that's left is to get it done, and the countdown has already started.

we had it all arranged and planned to perfection, it was just a matter of getting the green light from the F.B.I to make the move, then the order came to stop and shut it all down, I was working on my car at the time in the secret hide out when Ruby came and told me the news, I knew right there and then that Mr.Artmn has found out about it and stopped the whole thing, in my heart I just couldn't let it go that easy, I asked Ruby's boss if I can use their help off the record .

I needed some support from them if I'm going to bust Kevin and kill his operations, but we have to keep this between us, the man told me that he can't promise anything but he and his team will do the best they can, so working under the cover of night I went out, a man on a mission to run Kevin & his dad down, I had all the time in the world in prison to come up with this plan, the F.B.I in this case came as a bonus, so now the ball is in my court, time to get it rolling.

I asked Ruby to make a copy of Mr.Artmn's pictures and send them to him when I tell her with a note, warning him that if he makes a move to save Kevin copies of these picture will find its way to Mrs.Artmns hands and the media, I asked for a trailer that can carry me and my car, then I took a drive to see Cesar my supplier, he was shocked in a good way when his doorman told him I was outside his house door.

-Cesar-it's really you homz, I thought you were in jail.

-Me-I'm still in jail bro ...

he was puzzled a bit as we went inside but I wasted no time in persuading him to expand his actions and take Kevin's place coz he's about to go to jail, I asked him to find out who is Kevin's supplier in Mexico, and he told me that he knew the man, I asked him to go and meet with the man asap before someone steps in and take his place, so he can have first claim to this territory, also told him about some of what the guys in jail told me and what Kevin and his father were doing to some of our friends, and that he's selling drugs to school kids to make more profit .

Cesar is an old school dealer, he knew the rules of the game so he didn't like what he heard and he agreed with what I asked him to do, I told him to let me know when it's done, he gave me a phone and told me that he will get back to me in 2 or 3 days max, I think Cesar had this idea in mind for a long time but needed a reason to make his move and now he has it, Cesar didn't waste any time, after I left his place, he got on the next flight to California and crossed the border to mexico.

in the time I was waiting for Cesar, I fixed another plan with the F.B.I team, we had to keep it as simple as possible, coz after I do all this I had to get back to jail so I can get out legally, I finished working on my car I added the parts I got from Yoshi, we went to see amber at the hospital she was happy to see us, we checked her out and took her to ruby's place to stay with her until all this is done .

on the way back with ruby I got a message from Cesar saying that it's done, he even managed to stop the next shipment, that was my green light, I asked Ruby to call Kevin to see where he's at, turns out that he was on his way to the marina, I asked her to drop me off at my car, and call the police about some weird activity going on in the restricted area at the port and get the trailer rolling, it was close to midnight so I had to move fast .

when I got to the marina, I saw Kevin's Corvette parked and the trunk was open with some medium hand bags in it, I looked in the bags and found money in some and drugs in the others had drugs in them, Kevin was getting ready to sail to god knows where and was busy loading some diving gear on board, and there was a couple of hand bags similar to the ones in the car sitting there near his yacht waiting to be loaded on board, I thought that I can take a couple of those money bags from kevin's car to my car, so I did, then I walked towards him, and when I got close enough I said ...

-Me-hey Kevin, going on vacation??, by the looks of it I'd say you're heading to the Bahamas kid, they say it's amazing at time of the year.

He was surprised in a very bad way!!.
-Kevin-WTF !!... DJ I thought you were in jail !
-Me- I'm still in jail fool.
-Kevin-what?? .... How??
-Me-I came here to thank you for what you did to my workshop, you actually made me some money coz I had that place insured for a crazy amount of cash.

Then I got on the yacht while looking at him straight in the eye, he was backing up inside the yacht trying to get to his gun that was hidden somewhere as he was talking back to me...
-Kevin-you know what you are more than welcome my friend.
-Me-now I understand why you put me in jail coz I'm your friend, just like the rest of our friends serving time in there, that's a very bad habit Kevin but it was a good experience for me and I learned a lot ..
-Kevin-oh yea, like what??
-Me-I learned a few more things about you and your dad that's the good part, the bad part is you made me real angry, I'm going to make you pay for what you did to me, to Amber, to my workshop, and I'm going to beat it out of you .

he couldn't find his gun so he grabbed the nearest object to his hand then threw it at me, oh it's on now, I dodged it, the fight went down on the yacht, don't get me wrong Kevin has a few moves he can throw down when he has too, we wrecked the place, he fell over a closet and the emergency box dropped on the floor and the flare gun fell near his hand he grabbed it and shot at me.

I managed to get out of its way, the flare went all the way to the back of the yacht as we kept on fighting, I had the upper hand until I saw that the flare fell in the middle of the oxygen tanks,that's when I knew I had to get the hell out of there and in the nick of time we jumped out into the water as the tanks over heated and exploded destroying most of the yachts back end.

when I came up Kevin was closer to the dock and was climbing out I was I bit behind, he got to his car before me, and the chase was on, it looks like I blew out up his plan A in flames, now I think he's just trying plan B which is to get to the state line, at the this time of night the streets are almost empty, he thinks that he can run but not from me he can't, not tonigh, not even if his life depends on it, I wasn't in the mood to let that happen .

I used the voice dial to call Ruby, I told her what's going on and that I'm going to try to stop him in any way I can and to send someone to Mr. Artmn's house to deliver the pictures and the note, Mr. Artmn was in his office when he heard the door bell, he went to check who it was but there was no one there, just a file on his door step, when he opened it blood froze in his veins, stage one and two are on, stage three wasn't going to be easy knowing that Kevin is not thinking straight at this time, he is dangerous to himself and others on the road, a combination of a crazy man, a fast car and a gun is simply not a good one .

it was a race for life for both of us, I stayed on his tail and whenever I had a chance I pushed him to take certain exits towards the port to keep him boxed in when the police arrive, a police car spotted us and reported us in, a few minutes later things became interesting we have police cars on are tails and helicopters, police and local news, we kept going on that until I was successful in getting him in the port area, now I have to spin him or cut him off to give the police a chance to lock him in, there is only one way out for him now, an exit space that can only fit one car out, either me or him in an area full of shipping container and heavy machinery .

now it's a straight dash to that exit through heavy machinery, containers and other moving obstacles, a busy port is not the best place to do this, the problem is whenever I come close to him he shoots at me, I never could get as close as I need to spin his car around plus I don't want any of the port workers to get hurt,by now we're almost at the exit and I had one last chance, I waited for the right moment then I hit my nitrous to catapult my car ahead of him, now with a couple of turns to get to the exit point I flashed him with the rear flash light I had, it took him a second to recover from that to find himself going straight to a crane .

this is when he did the smartest thing he ever did, he turned the steering to spin the car around and hit the crane with the back of the car, and boom that chase ended in a cloud of white powder and money which he was caring in the back of his car covering my escape as I got to the exit through the dark zone of the port straight to the high way, by the time the cloud went away I was long gone, and the police has surrounded Kevin, he was in pain from the crash but nothing that can't be fixed, the police caught Kevin with enough evidence to send him to jail for a long time.

I called Ruby to tell me where to meet the trailer and she told me that Kevin's chop shop was raided by the police, all who were inside are under arrest now, she also said that the police found a big safe in the chop shop but it was empty, all they found was some traces of white powder in it, they took samples to be analyzed, I was so happy and high off my adrenalin rush that I was howling to the silver moon shining over the city, I made it to the meeting point and got into the trailer Michael knight style, and straight to back to jail,I went back in the same way I got out .

In the morning I was back in my cell, it took some time for things to happen, but finally Kevin got what he deserves, I saw him coming in the same day I was leaving jail, I smiled as I was leaving knowing that Kevin will have lots of fun in there, ruby was there to take me home, she was looking better than ever in a red mustang, on the way she told me that there is some one who wants to meet me, when I asked who she said you'll know later, I got home to my family and friends to find a welcome home BBQ celebration for me, I couldn't be any happier .

Ambers mom got out from jail, and amber had invested some of the money she got from Mrs.artmn in a small bakery shop with her mom and is planning on going to cooking school, ruby was awarded with the team she worked with for cracking this case, Kevin was learning to be really careful in jail and not dropping the soap in the shower, the police managed to find one of the two persons who set fire to my workshop from the security cameras flash drive that amber saved from the fire, they recognized a Taurus star sign tattoo on his arm coz he was wearing a t-shirt & a ski mask to cover his face, he confessed on the other guy and who put them up to it, so they joined Kevin to keep him company in jail .

the street king fest was coming soon so I need to get my work shop and life back together again, the companies that sponsored the street fest are helping me rebuild my workshop better than before as a thank you for all the profits that I helped them make through the street king fest, as for me well I'm what you can call top dog in this town now, my life was getting better and better every day and in every way and I'm enjoying every minute.

in case you're wondering about the bags, well let's say that dad now owns a nice boat and is a member of the yacht club, we sold the old house and moved out to a bigger one in the upper class side of town, and we all have platinum credit cards, thanks to my good friend Shawn, I forgot to mention that he is the manager in one of the local banks, he got the money in the bank no questions asked, and I helped him rebuild the green lantern back to its former glory.

I've done all I can do to finish this rivalry, but weird enough I still feel that it's not over yet, I don't know if Mr.artmn is going to let this go just yet, but he's going to have to live with it for a long time, and if you look in Mr.artmn's eyes you can really see it,my advice to you, if have hate in your heart against someone just let it go, a wise man once said it's like drinking poison and wishing the other person would die .

a couple of months later things cooled down and life was back to normal, my workshop was back to work, and we were getting ready again for the street king fest, I was talking to one of the guys about his car that was in my workshop, we were standing next to the car when I heard my phone playing that special ring tune that I kept for Ruby, she has been of the grid for too long,I told the guy I have to take this call and I'll be back in a minute, I picked up to hear these word (hey papi) .

-Me-hey sweet cheeks.

-Ruby-how you doing papi.

-Me-couldn't be better, how you been.

-ruby-oh can't complain, I had a vacation went to my family for a while,I just came back about 3 days ago, with you on my mind almost every day papi.

-Me- wow almost every day I'm flattered, so what's up, you miss the streets or what?

-Ruby-well not as much as I miss you, what are you doing tonight after 8 pm?

-Me-not much I close at 6 and go home, what do you have in mind?

-Ruby-did you rebuild the chill out?

-Me-better than before, I added a jacuzzi too.

-Ruby-cool, remember I told you there was someone who wants to meet you.

-Me-yea when you picked me up from jail, but you never said who it was.

-Ruby-well tonight you will know, I'll pick you up from the workshop at 8 pm ok, later papi.

she hung up and I felt a cold chill that ran down my spine, it felt good and weird at the same time, I looked at myphone watch and it was almost lunch time, I went back to finish the conversation with the car owner, an hour later work was done around the workshop, I gave my mechanics the rest of the day off and closed up then I went home for lunch,I just love moms cocking and today she made fried chicken, mash potato, greens and mushroom gravy, that meal knocked me out until night fall, I woke up to my phone ringing, it was ruby calling, it was a little after 8 I almost forgot my date, I answered the phone and she told me that she can't come pick me up and will send me a location to go to, she will meet me there in an hour .

I got my clothes on and had a light dinner by myself my brother was out, mom and dad are having dinner at a restaurant tonight, they're just enjoying their time now, sailing or fancy restaurants they even went to Hawaii twice so far, they are having fun and lots of it and who can blame them, that's why the house is empty most of the time now, and also that's why my mom wants to have grandkids soon, I don't know if I'm up for it yet, but she says that there is no better time than now, she keeps pushing me into it every day or trying to set me up on dates with some of her friends daughters, it's driving me crazy but in a good way .

I checked my phone and the location was there now it's time to get from point A to point B, now point B was in an old navy base that was closed years ago, when I got there I kept following the directions until I got inside the base, I saw a car tail light in a distance parked next to a spot light on the pear, I kept on driving towards it, when I got there I found ruby standing there, I parked next to her and after a warm welcome from my girl I heard heavy footsteps, sounded like a big man walking, I turned around to see a tall dark man walking towards us, then I heard ruby say DJ meet Atlas .

when he came into the light I was surprised to see the phantom guy I saw when I was in jail, it was really him, I tried to keep my cool and I just said ..
-Me-so the ghost has a name, a pleasure to finally meet you (as we shook hands)
-Atlas-good to see you again DJ, how's life treating you after jail?
-Me-good, getting better, what about you?
-Atlas-jail is not a place for someone like me DJ, I was there just to see what kind of man you are, and what are you made of, study your behavior, based on agent ruby's recommendation.

So I turned around at ruby looking for more details...
Ruby was about to explain when atlas interrupted and said allow me to explain.
-Atlas-both of you come with me I want to show you something.
We walked with Atlas into a dark building next to the peer, it looked like a workshop but all the machines inside looked old and rusty, they haven't been used in a long time, the place was barely lit, he told us to watch our step coz of the scattered old tolls and wires, I was looking around when atlas asked me

-Atlas-do you believe that we are the only intelligent life form in the universe DJ?
-Me- I think so, I haven't had an encounter with an Aline yet so yea I guess we're alone.
-Atlas-have you any idea about NASA's golden records?

we walked towards a small door on the other side of the building that had shelter writing on it, he opened the door with a magnetic card, we walked into a staircase that went down then walked in a long corridor, the place started to look like a scene from the movie men in black, the place was well lit and had a spacy feeling to it, then I said

-Me-so NASA is in the music business now?
-Atlas-no, the Voyager Golden Records are phonograph records that were included aboard both Voyager spacecrafts launched in 1977. The records contain sounds and images selected to portray the diversity of life and culture on Earth, and are intended for any intelligent extraterrestrial life form, or for future humans, who may find them. Those records are considered as a sort of a time capsule.
-Me-oh yea I heard about that but I didn't think it was real.
-Atlas-oh it's real, and we think that something out there actually found it. we reached a huge metal door with an eye scanner, and when he opened that door there was a small army of agents, big screens hanging from the ceiling, lots of desks with computers on them, I saw steaming videos of live coverage from street cams, and on the right there was the security center looking over this naval base, I couldn't imagine the amount of intel flowing into this place, I stood there for a minute just trying get my head around the whole scene, I turned around at ruby and she was just standing there as If this was an everyday thing then I heard Atlas say.
-Atlas-welcome to our headquarters under the sea, this is where we keep an eye on things.
-Me-what things?
-Atlas-come in, let me show you.
-Ruby- you want some coffee Papi?
-Me-yes please thanks.
-ruby- ok I'll back in a minute, you Listen very carefully to what atlas tells you ok Papi.

Ruby left to get the coffee, Atlas took me to one of the operators sitting behind a desk watching a screen, he was watching people dancing in a club having a good time, and I thought it was a movie, and then atlas said
-Atlas-do you see anything strange here?
-Me-everything looks normal to me, what am I looking for?

Then Atlas asked the operator to turn the spectrum filter on, then I started to see some Kind of stream of somesort of energy flowing from some of the people on the dance floor to other people who were chilling in the V.I.P and people that were at the bar, the stream was coming out of many people on the dance floor but going to a few that were absorbing it!.

-Atlas-do you see it now.
-Me-I do, what the hell is it?
-Atlas-human essence.
-Me-what??
-Atlas-the life energy that surrounds and flows from every one of us.
-Me-you mean these guys are feeding on it?
-Atlas-you can say that.
Then we went to another screen and another and another, and the same thing was going on, people were being drained of their life energy in deferent places, it was theft on a whole different level, then atlas started giving me more details.

-Me-how is this even happening?
-Atlas-where can I start, I asked you if you think that we are alone in this universe, I guess now you see that we are not, these are aliens living amoung us.

and as he went on talking ruby came back with the coffee and a light snack for me, it's like she read my mind, somehow I got the feeling that this chat is not going to end any time soon and it's going to be a long night, so the story turns out to be as atlas kept on talking.

-Atlas- people talk about UFO's and getting kidnapped by aliens, from what we know less than 5% of those stories are true, they did take some samples from the human race for examination purposes, they came back every once in a while for some reason beyond our understanding, maybe to get to know the planet a little bit better, or take more samples of the creatures that live on earth, animals, plants from different locations, I mean they scanned the whole planet from the north to the south pole, then the sightings stopped, no one was reporting night lights or strange encounters for a long time .

Then at the mid 90's an air force pilot was testing a new helmet for night combat noticed something strange over one of the cities near the testing grounds, a huge stream like the ones you saw on screen a few minutes ago but on a much larger scale, like a river flowing from the city to the sky all the way to the atmosphere well into space, he reported what he saw to the base even sent a video of what he saw, the military contacted a nearby observatory asking them if they can see anything over the area but they said no, Nasa was next on the list, they used their satellites to see what's going on, they managed to capture the stream flowing towards the southern end of the planet, they tried to get a satellite closer to that area but the stream just stopped and all they saw was just a flash like a shooting star speeding away into deep space .

then again nothing,monthes passed and investigations kept on going, trying to figure out what happened at that time, what was it and who was responsible, but all they came up with was just theories, we kept the satellites surveillance going and noticed short intervals of the same energy streams flowing from war or disaster hit areas, like they were taking whatever they can find without creating suspicions, still we couldn't catch an image of what their space ships look like, it was like they knew the second we try to see them they disappear .

more technology appeared and we were able to see what we were dealing with, the aliens were using an advanced level of stealth tech that's out of this world, but we are not stupid, by analyzing the energy stream spectrum we were able to see it going into the alien ship, track where it's been stored and get a glimpse of how they look like coz they consumed some of that energy, we found out that they use our bio energy as food and fuel for their ships.

again they disappeared, I guess they knew that we saw them, time passed months, years and still nothing, we thought at the time that they vanished, this time they took the time to evolve themselves to take the form of human beings, someone suggested we use the ultra-vision energy tracking technology at ground level and to our surprise there they were, hiding among us in human form, now they had the balls to steal from us face to face, the matters got hotter when we found casualties, bodies that were examined by the police and reported the cause of death as drugs overdose .

there was so many of them the police didn't bother to do an autopsy on all of them specially after a big gatherings like the burning man fest, then the numbers increased as more casualties were found in and around the cities, so we sent our team to take another look at the bodies, what we found was shocking, some of them had smaller internal organs, shrunken hearts, livers and kidneys, extremely low fluid content, their blood was almost as thick as jell or in some cases almost powder form.

based on that we started to send agents into these gatherings using the ultra-vision technology in hidden in cameras, and there we found aliens hiding in plain sight among the crowd, before taking action our agents sent us videos of what they saw, then atlas showed me some videos, these aliens actually look like normal people to the naked eye except when you look at them with ultra-vision cameras, then you notice that they have a greenish glow in the white of their eyes, the party looks normal until we saw some persons in the videos walking around talking to people offering them a strange formula, they tell them it's a new type of drug, a new high, all it takes is a few drops in the persons drink or directly in the mouth and it takes you to happy land, sometimes they just secretly put a few drops in someone's drink without telling them, and in a few minutes that person gets so hyped up like it's his birthday and goes on partying like crazy, dancing the night away.

without the ultra-vision camera you just see a man or a woman dancing the hell out of themselves, which is normal in a place like that, but with the ultra-vision you see that persons ora just lighting up like a xenon light, then when that happens the aliens pass by that person get a whiff then stand at distance of a few matters away and just breath that persons energy, sometimes the victim is shared by 2 or more aliens just chilling and sipping away, when the morning comes some of these victims collapse others survive depending on how much of their energy has been drained and how healthy that person is to start with, we don't know how the aliens pick their victims, is it random or do they see something we don't.

we were not sure if they were doing this anywhere else but we have to clean up our house first, the president gave us his permission to start this secret task force for a single purpose, catch or kill these aliens where ever and whenever we can using top technology with the help of others which I can't

give you names of like the guy that wears the red iron suit that can fly, and
our friends the alien robots that can change shape who helped us with some
technology and info about these aliens we are hunting.

our good fortune brought us a step closer to these aliens when the D.E.A
busted a drug lord and found in his possession a strange drug in a small
bottle,they brought the dealer in for interrogation and when he started
spilling the beans, it turned out to be the same stuff the aliens use on
their victims, we found out that this drug is actually manufactured in labs
which were owned by him and other partners, his story was that he was
approached by some strangers from out of town a few years ago, and they
offered him a formula and the raw key material to produce a new kind of
drug, no trace in the users blood and no health side effects, a pure high
that goes whichever way the user likes, they called it Slip Dream, they said
they couldn't afford to do it themselves coz of financial issues, so the drug
lord reached to an agreement with these strangers on how things would
go about making and selling this new drug, the strange part he said was it
was an easy agreement as if they were not very interested in the financial
profit as much as the distribution of the drug.

When we told him that we might be able make a deal with him, he opened
up to even more details, he told us that the raw material the strangers
brought to him was something he never saw before, it was like a matter that
came from out of this world, a solid red crystals that had a green glow, they
brought a new amount every 2 to 3 months, these crystals melt in liquid
nitrogen, huge amounts of nitrogen was used every time we make a new
batch, then It was mixed with pure THC, but when it was tested they found
it was too strong, some of the test subjects had a near death experience,
they tried a few other strands of weed untill they mixed it with pure sativa
extract and it proved to be the right mix, when that is done it turns to a light
green fluid, it was one of the strangest things he ever saw, later it had to sit
out in the early morning sun from dawn for about 3 to 4 hours then it turns
pink, that meant it's ready, then it gets stored in a refrigerator ready to be
bottled in small plastic containers and sold to consumers, it can be carried
around airports or borders and doesn't raise any kind alerts.

the long tour almost came to its end and atlas kept on talking as ruby and
I were walking with him through the place, we reached his office and went

inside, I finished my sandwich and I was sipping on what's left of my coffee, he offered us a drink and I said no thank you but ruby said she'll have one, I felt that he had a little bit more to tell, and sure as hell he did, as he sat down behind his desk and said .

-Atlas-the drug lord also confessed to a few laboratories in and around the city which we raided and closed but no luck of finding the raw crystals, we made a deal with the drug lord to help us catch the strangers in exchange for the reduction of his jail time pulse some privileges in his jail cell, but the drug lord was killed a few days after he was released from jail, putting us back where we started.

A few days later one of our agents was killed, then another one killed in a car accident, we lost over a dozen agents in one month, we knew we were being hunted down, over the next few weeks we lost so many of our men and women, it was when our main headquarters was attacked that's when we knew that it was one of our agents who sold us out to the aliens and the drug dealers, he hacked into our system and exposed the agents names and information, the drug lords put a bounty on them, they got hunted down by every junky that had a gun on the street, the agents name is Patrick Solomon code name the surgeon, navy seals tactics expert,he exposed our whole operation to the aliens and the drug dealers costing us huge loses in lives and resources, some of us managed to escape and others fought until the bitter end .

It took just an hour to breach our old headquarters, he had the guts to come in from the main gate to the heart of it, they killed every one who stood in their way in cold blood we saved what we could of what we had of info and gear and went underground for a while to recover from this crisis, all of our agents came from military backgrounds, army, navy, special forces, some of the best, but it wasn't enough when that agent brought an army of Aline's and drug dealers henchmen with Alien tech weapons against us, we were over taken by sheer numbers, they killed as many as they could of our people before taking over our headquarters, the surgeon had this attack planned down to the smallest detail, it took us a couple of years to come back to what you see here, it wasn't easy .

-Me-wow, man that's an epic story, but no one explained to me why am I here or what did ruby recommended me for yet .

-Atlas-aah yes, like I said earlier we are back, we had enough of watching what's going on, and we are ready to take action, I asked agent ruby to join us based on the recent bust of Kevin Artmn, we thought it her work until she told us the whole story, and that it was your planning and execution, in our line of work I need someone like you.

-Me-need someone like me, as in you want me to work with you guys??

-Atlas- yes .

-Me- yes?!.

-Atlas- yes .

-Ruby- it will be fun, we can work together papi .

-Me-work?! ... Have Fun doing what?

-Atlas-after what I saw in jail, and how you handled you self throughout your sentence, no fights no enemies, inmates trusted and respected you, plus you're a street racer, and you got connections with some of the local dealers, you're the perfect man for the job.

-Me-what job??

-Atlas- an agent of the ATF

-Me-what is the ATF?

-Atlas-Alien Termination Force.

-Me-you want me to kill aliens??

-Ruby-and catch or kill the surgeon papi.

-Me-you do know that I have no military experience right.

-Atlas-that's one of the main reasons that makes you the right man for the job, you have no history in the system, you can be a ghost.

-Me-that drink must have went straight to your heads.

-Atlas-ruby talk to your man.

-Ruby- papi

-Me- sweet cheeks this not for me

-Atlas-sweet cheeks!

-Ruby-these people need a saviour.

-Me-I'm not a super hero or Jesus.

-Atlas-we can give you some super powers DJ.

-Me-what do you mean you can give me super powers?.

-Atlas-a new technology, nanobots that attach themselves to strategic points on your muscles and nerve system giving you faster reflexes,skills, speed,and power, you'll be connected to our tracking system and we can load you up with almost any skills you might need in any situation, making you the perfect assassin.

-Me- an assassin?!!!!

-Atlas-I meant hunter, our idea is to have one great hunter to cut the snakes head and deliver results, like the Japanese yakuza one assassin for the organization that takes out whoever they need to kill, you can have your normal everyday life and we will call you when we need you .

-Me-hunter or whatever, it's not for me, can't do it, I'm not a killer, never killed anyone, hope I never have too .

-Atlas-you don't have to kill humans they are just aliens, not even animals, and they are killing humanity.

-Me-in any way they are god's creation, as far as I know he created everything and everyone, I'm sorry atlas but I don't think that I'm the man for this job .

We all went quiet for a moment, atlas gave me that I need you to change your mind look and spoke to me in a deep voice, he said...

-Atlas-this is for humanity, unless you chose to do this I can't force you in to it.

-Me-thank you sir, it was a pleasure to meet you but I have to excuse myself and leave if you don't mind.

-Atlas-not at all, thank you for taking the time to be here and being a good listener, I was really looking forward to working with you, I have to ask you to never mention anything about this place or what you know to anyone .

-Me-don't worry your secret is safe with me, you have my word.

We shock hands, and he escorted us out of the building, and just before we exit the last door atlas said

-Atlas-this job would have changed the way you live forever, many things you know will change, extreme adventure is the name of this game.

-Me-I had a feeling you might say something like that, but I don't go extreme unless I really have to, I think my life is exiting enough for now, thanks again for your time and hospitality and I hope you find the right man for the job soon .

Atlas lit up his cigar and went back inside, ruby and I walked back to our cars, she asked me if I was hungry?

-Me-sure

-Ruby-what do you have in mind?

-Me-I needs some soul food, then we can order dinner, what do you think about that.

-Ruby-ooh I got plenty of food for you soul papi, I'm in the mood for some Italian food tonight,can you pick it up on your way back, I got something special for your eyes only back at my place, I'll get it and I'll meet you back at your workshop in an hour ok .

-Me-sounds good to me.

I just got to admit I love watching that Chicca walking away twisting that slim waist side to side, keeping that image in mind I got in my ride and drove back,all the way back I kept thinking about what I saw back there, the idea of aliens living among us!, I couldn't believe what I saw, is it really happening, what kind of world are we living in and what is it coming to, if we actually have aliens sharing our planet with us, and feeding on us too, what went wrong in this universe that moved us a step lower in the food chain.

I was really hungry on the way back, it's a good thing that kept a chocolate bar in the car, coz after the 2 hours that we spent with atlas I was about to take a bite off my arm, that snack that ruby got me was like a diet sandwich, I got the food and went straight back to my workshop, I went upstairs and put some mood music on, I had a quick shower and rolled one smoked it and laid down in my bed waiting for ruby to get here,I think I dosed off for about an hour or less coz it was almost 12.30 am when I woke up to the phone, it was ruby calling asking me to let her in, I can sincerely say that by morning I had a slight case of amnesia, it took me a while to remember what went on last night I almost believed that my real name was papi.

days and weeks went by, life was good and my workshop was doing great, we were coming up to almost the end of summer, the weather was starting to get cooler and soon we will start preparing for the street king fest again, with all the things that happened lately time just flew by so fast, it felt like the last fest just finished yesterday, my brother is almost 18 now and just started collage, and the good thing is he chose a collage near home, he still lives with us so mama doesn't need to worry about him, and she keeps giving me a hard time about why I'm still single, talking about she wants grandchildren pronto .

lately every once in a while we get visits from one of moms friends with her daughter, and when I walk in the house, I fall in the same trap every time, DJ come meet my friend and her daughter, sit down have some tea, then they twist whatever subject they were talking about to home life and settling down, nothing is greater than family life, watching your kids grow, then they talk about this girl and how good her cocking is, how she takes good care of home, and how she might make a very lucky man happy someday, I can't say that I hated them all, but a home girl would suffer with the way I live my life now, one time mom said why don't you marry that nice girl Amber I like her, mom I love you but I'm not ready to slow down yet.

it's that time again, and the street fest is on, thanks to my two favorite girls Amber and Ruby, we got this show on fire again, we had some cases that people went to hospital during the fest parties for health or other reasons, but now after what atlas showed me I started to pay more attention to what's going on, one night when I was on stage doing my thing on the turn tables my brother Darrell came up and asked me for the keys to my trailer, he said he will bring it back in an hour, I gave him the keys and kept on doing what I'm doing, I was trying to see if I can spot anything like what atlas showed me on screen back at the base, but I couldn't notice any weird activity going on .

about 30 minutes later the next DJ came on stage, I picked up my stuff and went straight to my trailer coz I really needed to use the bathroom, when I got close to the trailer I knocked on the door but there was no answer I opened the door and called my brother's name but he didn't answer,I went into the bathroom done my thing and got out then went to bed room to check, the door was half open I saw some clothes on the floor, I walked in and got the shock of my life, my brother flat on his back on the bed, eyes barely open and almost out of breath, when he saw me he couldn't even move a muscle, I jumped on the bed and I tried to get him to sit up, he looked at me and said in a fading voice ..

-Darrell-help me bro.
-Me-what happened to you, who did this, Darrell, Darrell, stay with me bro
-Darrell- I'm tired bro,can't move, i just want to sleep.

I called for the medical team, ruby and amber saw the medical team on the move and followed them to see what was wrong, they were shocked when they saw that it was my trailer, those were the longest minutes of my life as I waited for the medics to arrive, our life flashed in my head, since we were kids until now.

Darrell was going in and out of consciousness as I kept shouting at him and shaking him to stay awake and just a few seconds before the medic team arrived his eyes rolled up and he wasn't breathing any more, I screamed his name as loud as could, the medics pulled him out of my hands by force and held me down, coz I was going out of my mind, they tried CPR but it didn't work, his pulse is fading and with every second that pass the risk of losing my brother increases, a minute later the ambulance arrived they put him inside and they shocked him and nothing happened, they gave him an adrenaline injection and still nothing, then the increased the voltage and shocked Darrell again, but still the flat line on the screen didn't change, they gave up on him, I jumped in the ambulance and held his head and said this in his ear.

-Me-whoever or whatever did this to you I swear to god I will make them regret the day they were born, I promise you, but I want you to be there to see it, so if your still there and you can hear me wake up .

then I shook him hard and I screamed wake up of the top of my lungs, when the medic next to him saw this, he yelled clear and shocked him one more time, we all turned to the screen and suddenly we heard a peep, his pulse is back but he was still unconsciousness, my eyes were burning in tears that I just couldn't control, now we have hope, Amber went in ambulance with Darrell and asked me to stay behind until I calm down and told me she'll keep me posted on any updates, they rushed him to the hospital .

I went back inside the trailer, rinsed my face with cold water several times in the bathroom, went back to the bed room to lay down for a few minutes coz I was feeling a bit light headed, I sat down on the bed just trying to focus, I started to recall what just happened, that's when Ruby came in, she hugged me and said

-Ruby-are you ok papi?

-Me-I'll be ok when my brother gets better, I just can't believe what just happened, it just doesn't make sense.
-Ruby-everyone gets tiered of work some times.
-Me- yes but not like this, Darrell was totally exhausted he was barely able to speak, he couldn't lift a finger.
-Ruby-is he diabetic or what??
-Me-no not Darrell, my brother is an athlete,he was on the football team in high school and now he got a scholarship to collage because of football, a very energetic kid, he looked a bit older than his age.
-Ruby-how old is he?
-Me-almost 18
-Ruby-I thought he was a few years older.
-Me-I think my mom fed him better than me, one of the reasons that I work out is so he doesn't start to think that he can beat me up some day, he is all about a healthy life style, no alcohol or energy drinks, which makes me almost sure that he is not just exhausted from helping us organize the fest this year, and when he came and asked me for the key he looked ok.
-Ruby-was he alone?
-Me-I don't know, coz he said he'll bring the keys back in an hour, we need to check the security cams.

while I was talking to ruby I turned to my left and found a plastic cup next to the bed with some beverage left in it, about a quarter left, it was some soft drink with no alcohol in it,I knew this was my brothers drink coz I saw this cup in his hand when he took the key from me, and like me he doesn't drink alcohol,I started to have my doubts, could it possibly have Slip Dream in it?.
-Ruby-what is it papi?
-Me-I don't know but I hate to think that this drink might have you know what in it.
-Ruby-you mean Slip Dream?
-Me-yep, can you contact atlas?
-Ruby-sure.
-Me-I need you to take this to him to get it analyzed asap, just to make sure, I'm going to go to the security center to check the cams, then go to the hospital, let me know as soon as you find out anything ok .
-Ruby-you got it papi, just take care of yourself get some rest before you leave, I'll see you later tonight.

Ruby left in a hurry and I went to the security center to see what was my brother up to, with the help of the man in charge we managed to see Darrell going to the trailer with a couple of hot chicks, I mean booming bodies, wearing tight apple bottom torn jeans and cut t-shirts, it was hard to see how they looked like coz one was wearing a baseball cap and the other had long hair covering her face blocking the camera view, 30 minutes later on the security tape the girls left the trailer in a hurry, as they came out they kept looking down as if they knew where exactly the security cameras were, I think I might have passed by those girls on my way to the trailer I couldn't see their faces coz it was a bit dark in that spot, they were walking towards the exit to the car parking area to my right, I was only saw their back side as they were walking away .

I took a copy of the security disk and got in my car then drove to the hospital, on the way all I was thinking about was how can I tell my parents about this, thank god that they were in Hawaii for the next couple of weeks, and if I'm lucky Darrell will get better before they come back, it's been a little over 2 hours since they took Darrell to the hospital, the time was getting close to midnight,
When I arrived at the hospital I found Amber standing outside talking on the phone and walking in a circle, when she saw me she covered the mic and whispered...

-Amber-shhh, it's your mom
-Me-ooh shit!!

I checked my phone and found my mom's number, with other missed calls, I started to believe what they say about a moms heart it knows when something goes wrong, but wait a minute why didn't she call when I got arrested ?!,I need to talk to her about this when she gets back, Amber finished the phone call and turned to me and took my hand and walked inside the hospital to Darrell's room, as we were walking she said .

-Amber-god it's so hard to lie to your mom, how do you guys do it?
-Me-we don't, what did you tell her, and how's Darrell?
-Amber-I told her you were rocking he crowed, I sent her a video that I shot of you earlier, and Darrell left his phone with me in the security center on

the charger, the doctors say he's ok he just needs to sleep, they gave him an IV with some nutrients, he should be better by morning .

we got Darrell's room, I looked in through the door glass to see him sleeping like a baby, with monitors and an iv attached to him,when the doctor came out of Darrell's room I asked him about Darrell's condition, he said he suffered high exhaustion and lack of fluids coz his blood was a bit thicker than usual, they took a blood sample to the lab to examine it and they didn't find any trace of any kind of drugs, they gave him a glucose iv with vitamins, and later when he wakes up they will give him a light meal, he is stable for now and his vital signs are normal, they will keep an eye on him for now and will notify me of any changes, they were not sure when will he wake up, coz sometimes deep sleep is the bodies way of healing it self, the doctor told me not to worry, he doesn't know that I need Darrell to call mom or it's my ass on the line .

Amber and I went to a small Greek restaurant near the hospital, we sat down to get something to eat, I wasn't feeling hungry but I knew I had to eat something, coz of what happened earlier I was feeling a nasty burn in my stomach, I ordered a lite appetizer cucumber mixed with yogurt, a couple of bites into it and I started to feel better, I guess my stomach acid was too high coz of the mental state I was in, even after what the doctor told me I can't help but worry and the scene kept running over and over in my mind, we sat there quietly slowly eating our meals until our silence was interrupted by my phone ringing, it was ruby, I picked up .

-Me-talk to me.
-Ruby- I'm at the hospital papi where are you.
-Me-Amber and I are in the Greek resonant across the street for the hospital.
-Ruby- the test results from atlas confirmed that Darrell's drink had Slip Dream in it and you should come here papi, Darrell woke up and the nurse is giving him some soup .

I couldn't believe what I just heard, I got up and put some money on the table and told Amber that Darrell woke up, we ran to the hospital, we went to his room and there he was, getting hand fed like a little boy by the nurse, we shook hands but I couldn't help hugging him hard, and he was trying to act cool in front of everybody ....

-Darrell-come on now chill, it's not a big deal bro...

I found my self looking deep into his eyes, like it was the first time I see him after years of being apart, my eyes were burning with tears of joy, I felt that the world just lit up again, it was like I'm looking at my new born child, I forgot that ruby, amber, the nurse and the doctor were standing there watching, every one saw how a big softy I became, at that moment it was just Darrell and I, when I turned at them they all had a smile on their faces, they all saw my happy daddy face, now Ruby and Amber are giggling, so I broke the silence.
-Me- junior you don't know the half of it, we'll talk about this in the morning ok bro.
He smiled pulled me close and whispered in my ear
-Darrell-you didn't have to call me junior in front of the ladies just now.
-Me-ooh ma bad, a slip of the tongue bro, hope I didn't ruin anything?
-Darrell-I was just about to get the nurses phone number man.
-Me- what?,I thought you already did, you're getting slow bro.

we bumped fists and as I was getting ready to leave the doctor walked with me outside then told me that my brother is one tough kid, but they have to keep him in for a couple more days just to make sure that everything is ok, I said you can keep him for the rest of the week just make sure that there is no long term damage, money is not an issue when it comes to family,I shook the doctors hand and was on my way out of the hospital, the girls caught up with me at the car parking, Amber said she has to go home get a good night sleep coz I asked her to look over things at the fest in the morning, Ruby looked like she had something to say and after Amber left she said.

-Ruby-we need to talk papi.
-Me-tell me, what do you have in mind.
-Ruby-not here.
-Me-ok I'm going to get some food on my way back to the workshop meet me there, you want me to get you anything?
-Ruby-I'm good papi, I'll see you there.

on the way back I kept thinking about what just happened, and that it happened in my town and to my brother of all people, it was a bit too much to handle, thank god that Darrell is ok, but still nobody gets away with hurting a member of my family, and I promised my brother that whoever did this to him is going to pay for it.

When I got to my place I had a long shower,then i got started on my meal and, minutes later I got a message from Ruby thet says (we're outside), I asked (who's we ?), she said (atlas is with me),that girl has just messed up my plan for the night !, I went down stairs to let them in, we went upstairs .
-Me-coffee anyone?
-Ruby-no thanks.
-Atlas-yes please.
-Ruby-I'll get it,you can finish your meal papi.
-Atlas- sorry about what happened to your brother, I hope he's feeling better.
-Me-yea thank god for that, he's a good kid he didn't deserve what happened to him.
-Atlas-he's one tough kid and lucky to have a brother like you, many don't survive something like that, so DJ how does it feel to know that you could have stopped this from going down in your town and to your own brother?
-Me-I know what you're trying to do, to make a long story short if you want me in your operation, you need to know that I do things my way .
-Atlas-and what exactly is your way, do you have a plan already?
-Me-not yet, I need a few days, and if I need your help I'll let you know.
-Atlas-oh you will need my help and a lot of it, just do me a favor don't do anything crazy before you talk to me or Ruby understand ?.
-Me-number 1 you're not my boss, number 2 I don't do crazy.

atlas stood there for a second looking at me, I don't know what went through his mind, maybe he was having second thoughts I'm not sure, but I just couldn't read that look in his eyes, did he see something in me that I didn't see in myself, what ever it was he kept it to himself.

-Atlas-I hope your brother gets well soon, good night DJ, we'll let you finish your meal and get some rest.
-Ruby-good night papi, don't worry Darrell will be just fine.

she left with atlas and I went to sleep a few minutes after,next morning the first thing I did was go see how Darrell was doing, I walked into the room with breakfast in my hand to find my old friend Cesar in the room with

Darrell, he arrived just a few minutes before me, how lucky can I be, just the man I wanted to see, after breakfast, Cesar and I went outside for a walk in a small garden near the hospital, we sat on a bench under a tree, it was nice sunny day, then I asked him ...

-Me-hey how did you know that my brother is here, I didn't tell anyone about it coz I don't want my parents to know .
-Cesar-from my baby cousin Rosita remember her, she use to have a crush on you back at the day,she's a nurse at the hospital, last night was her shift, and she was the nurse in charge of looking after your brother, she called me and told me late last night .
-Me-that was her, little rosy, my god she changed a bit, I thought I knew her when she was in the room but I wasn't sure .
-Cesar-yea homz she's married with 2 kids now.
-Me-wow, how the years pass so fast, any way did you hear anything about a new drug going around these days?
-Cesar-it's funny that you ask I was just about to ask you about the same thing homz, what do you know about it?
-Me-from what I heard it's like an express way to dream land, clean no side effects, doesn't leave a trace in the body, easy to move around check points, that's about it.
-Cesar-you tried it?
-Me-no man, did you?
-Cesar-not me homz deno my test subject you remember him right?
-Me- is that guy still alive? Man where did he get it from?
-Cesar-a guy in a grey suit and dark glasses came to me a few weeks ago, his name was Felix carter, he asked me if I can supply him with a crazy huge amount of pure sativa no mixed strands, and he gave me an offer to sell this new drug, as a soul dealer for this state, when I asked about what it was he told me exact same stuff you just said, and when he asked me to try it I said no man, but I'll find someone who would, I asked deno to try it out .
-Me- ok.
-Cesar-felix put a couple of drops on deno's tongue, deno said it tastes like lemonade, felix wrote his number on a piece of paper and asked me to contact him on this number then left, a minute later my boy deno was smiling,singing, dancing, having the time of his life, like it was his birthday, when I asked him about how he felt, he said I feel like I'm on top of the world, like I'm 15 again, this lasted for a few hours, after that he was back

to normal no headache or hangover effect and in a good mood too, now I know a that only a hand full of guys grow pure sativa around here and in the sates around us, everybody else just do mixed breeds .
-Me-you sound like you going to take the deal.
-Cesar-I didn't give felix an answer that day, it's a good deal but my hands are full right now and to open a new market for this is going to take some effort to control.
-Me-I want it
-Cesar-wait you didn't tell me how you knew about this drug, what you don't share with Cesar any more.
-Me-you won't believe what you're going to hear but I want your word that this stays between us only.
-Cesar-you got my word I swear on my mother's honor homz.

I told Cesar that I met a dealer in prison who was caught and this drug was found on him, and the dealer told me about the strangers that came to him with the raw material the drug is made of and how it's made .

-Me-at first I didn't believe what the guy in prison told me, but now after what I heard from you the game changed, I need you to get me in contact with all of these sativa growers, I want a piece of the action .
Cesar went silent for a minute then he said

-Cesar-you got it homz, I'll text you the numbers, tell them that I sent you, and you won't have any problems,if you need anything else you come to me first ok .
-Me-thanks man that makes us even.

We shook on it, and then he said he had to go take care of some business, I walked with him to his car, I was looking around for his ride a convertible classic Chevy but I couldn't find it, so I asked him

-Me-you still drive that cool Chevy, where is it, I don't see it around here, did you park it behind the hospital?
-Cesar-Na homz that's old news I got a new ride now, here it comes now.

we were standing in front of the hospitals main gate when a convertible Bentley pulled over, with a driver and a couple of hot Latinas in the back seat, he got in the car, sat in the middle,and one of the girls poured him a glass of chilled champagne, I stood there smiling as he waved good bye and left, it was then when I remembered that I should have asked for a percentage when I gave him Kevin's business,I went inside to check up on Darrell and I found him sleeping, so I thought I go check out what's going on with Amber at the fest, I bought lunch for us and went there, when I got there I called Amber and asked her to meet me at my trailer for lunch .

She came in 15 minutes later just after they closed the track coz it's high noon and it was getting too hot to race, so everyone get some rest and get ready for the night races, we sat down and she gave me a quick rundown about today's events over lunch, after lunch I went to bed for a nap coz I had to go back to the hospital later, I opened my eyes couple of hours later to find amber spooning me, to say the truth it took me back to the sweet old days before Kevin and all this happened, just felt so good to feel her arms around me, and it has been a while since I had some soul food.

I woke up smiling which is something that I haven't done in a long time, I started the coffee machine,and went to the bathroom, when I came out Amber was sitting on the side of the bed putting her jeans on,I made us some coffee and gave her one as she came out of the bedroom and asked her

-Me-are you doing anything after you're done with the fest?
-Amber-I don't think so, why, what do you have in mind?
-Me-I'll be at the hospital with Darrell, I need you to pick up Darrell's car from the detailing shop, put it on a trailer and send it to my house please, I'll be there to receive it after I leave the hospital and call me when you finish your work here let's have dinner and chill a bit at the workshop like the old days, if you're free later.
-Amber-sounds good babe, take care I'll call you as soon as I'm done here.

a hug and a simple kiss, and she left back to the fest, I didn't finish my coffee coz I didn't want to miss visiting hours at the hospital, at the hospital in Darrell's room the doctor came in to do the evening check up on Darrell, the doctor said that all vital signs are good, and maybe Darrell can leave the hospital tomorrow or the day after, it was like sweet music to my ears.

I had some time alone with Darrell after the doctor left the room, and I wanted to know how this happened to him...

-Me-ok tell me what happened, who are these chicks and where did you meet them.
-Darrell-you want to try your luck with them too?, here check this out I got a selfie with them at the coffee shop.

we laughed about it, exchanged a few jokes about it, a minute later I asked him again and he started telling me what happened

-Darrell-it was my break time so I went to check on my ride at Tim's detailing near the coffee shops, I got there and found my car outside the shop getting the final touch ups, the detailing guy told me that my car will be ready within the hour, these two hot chicks were chilling on a table in the coffee shop facing where my car was, I was checking out my ride and looked over and noticed that they were looking my way, then the one wearing a baseball cap came over and said hi I'm Tania, is this your car, I said yes, she started to ask about the car how big is the engine, performance, fuel economy that kind of stuff and I was answering, she went on walking around the car looking inside, making moves showing off her body, leaning over showing what she got, and brother the girl got it going on and her perfume was out of this world, then she says why don't you come join us, meet my girl carmen, I thought things couldn't get better .

I sat down with them, she introduced me to her friend carmen, she asked me if I would like something to drink, I said I'll have whatever your having, and she said it's a special blend from her friend that works in the coffee shop, I said cool hook me up, a couple of minutes later she came back with the drink and things were going great, bro that drink tasted real good and I felt like a million dollars, like I was living my best dream at the time, then they started to get naughty,they came real close to me, one on my right and the other on my left they started making moves under the table, touching and rubbing on my legs I thought this was my lucky night .

I asked them if they were free later, then the one wearing the cap Tania said there is no better time than now coz they were leaving town in a few hours, that's when I came to you to get the keys to the trailer, we went in and they said we got something special for you, lay down and enjoy the show, I got on the bed and got some music on the stereo and they started dancing, touching and rubbing on each other, stripping one another, I mean the whole nine yards bro,a few minutes later I started to feel a bit strange, I thought maybe I was a little tired from running around but I can't back down now .

They got on the bed next to me, and took my shirt off and went on kissing and licking on my body, I felt my heart bumping like I was running for a touchdown, then suddenly everything started slowing down, my heart beats went down, I couldn't feel my arms or legs any more, I was fighting to keep my eyes open and get air in my lungs, that's when they stopped and got off me and started to put their clothes on in a hurry, last thing I remember about them was Tania saying we are so sorry sweetness we didn't mean any harm, and they left me there fighting for my life, thank god you came when you did, that's all I remember bro, next thing I know is waking up here .

-Me-thank god you made it through this bro, otherwise mom would kill me.

-Darrell-why what happened?

-Me-nothing!

-Darrell-WHAT?!, what do you mean nothing?

-Me-the doctor said you were dehydrated and maybe a bit exhausted that's all, and recommended that you get some rest for the next few days, that means that no more work for you at the fest ok bro.

-Darrell-for real, come on man...

-me-you did more than enough bro, besides it's a couple of days and the fest will be done,so don't worry about it, I got this, just focus on getting better now ok .

I was saved at that moment when they brought his dinner and I got a message from Cesar that contained the phone numbers that I asked for, finally I can get things going, I couldn't tell Darrell what happened to him that night, it would dramatize him on the long run, maybe even have an effect on his future in football, from my point of view it's better he doesn't know about what really happened for now, I gave him his phone and told him not to tell mom that he is in the hospital, she doesn't know plus I don't want my parents to worry, what they don't know won't hurt them right ?.

I left the hospital and I had some time on my hands, I went by the house to check on things, the trailer driver called me up to tell me that he's outside the house with Darrell's car, I got the car parked in the house garage went back inside had a shower and got some clean clothes, left the house passed by the Italian restaurant to get a meal for me and Amber later, by the time I got to the garage amber came in a few minutes later, we sat down for a late dinner, we talked about the fest I told her that I'm going on a road trip after the fest to set up a few deals and she asked if she can come along, to say the truth I can use some company on this trip, after that we got buzzed cuddled on the sofa bed to watch a movie and fell asleep shortly after, I had some naughty ideas for the night, but when I saw how tired Amber was I just had to be a gentleman and change my plans .

next morning as usual Amber went to the fest and I woke up a bit later to a message from Darrell saying that the doctor said he can leave today, I was happy to know that he is well enough to come back home before my parents get back, I went out straight to the hospital to bring Darrell back home, I met the doctor in charge, I asked him a few questions about Darrell's condition, what he can and can't do for the next few day, the doctor Said Darrell shouldn't do much physical work for a few days meaning no football workout other than that just rest have good meals and his medication,I have to make sure that he looks at his best when mom and dad come home,I finished the paper work required and we left the hospital an hour later,by the time we got home it was almost noon, we ordered pizza for lunch, later I went to the fest to check on things, and Darrell stayed home like the doctor ordered .

the next day we were done with the fest and crowned a new street king in our closing party, everybody is happy, 24 hours later my parents came home, everything was cool and mom found everything like she left it in excellent shape, now it's time for Amber and I to hit the road,and get the deals done, ruby disappeared for the past few days no calls or messages, her mobile has been turned off since the night she came with atlas to the workshop, I only can get in touch with atlas through ruby and now both of them are off the grid, all I can do is hope that she's not doing something stupid, for the short time I knew that girl I know she would get in some kind of trouble head first .

I spent the next day making sure everything is ok at home and get my things ready, now I'm good to go, I told the family about the road trip the next day then I picked up Amber and hit the road, we looked like a couple on a honey moon trip, I needed some time out and this was the perfect chance, we had some fun on and off the road if you know what I mean, Amber really fed my soul, we did the deals and got great prices too, with Amber there these guys just lose focus when they look at her angelic eyes and hot body, they become soft and easy to bargain with, which was good for me, I asked them to let me know as soon as the harvest is done so I can get it transferred, and if any one comes buying they should send him to me .

I had to keep Amber in the dark about the real purpose of this trip, 2 weeks into our trip and we were done, the trip was successful on every level,it was just great to have some one on one time with Amber and I mean that literally, now that we are safely home there was nothing more to do but to get back to our daily business and wait, 2 weeks went by before I got word from some of the growers that the crops were ready, I told them that I will send them transports to bring the produce in asap, I already have found a good storage place thanks to Cesar and got it prepared, it was an adventure to bring it in the weed through state lines under the star lights, we had to use hidden routs, fast cars, play shadow games with cops, bribe some inspectors to overlook extra Wight on a few trailers, for ten days I did whatever that was possible to make this happen, the amount was huge, and I have spent too much money and effort to get it done, losing was not an option.

three days after this went down, at around 6 pm, I was doing some final check up on a car at my work shop all by myself, all my mechanics had left an hour ago, I was almost done when my phone rang, it was Cesar so I picked up ..

-Me-what's up C?
-Cesar-hey homz, you busy later tonight?
-Me-Na man, just about to close up shop and go home, what's going on?
-Cesar-why don't you come over for dinner?
-Me-dinner, where at?
-Cesar-at my new place home, you need to come check it out, I got some guests coming too.

-Me-any one I know?

-Cesar-Na homz, guests from out of town.

-Me-this should be fun, can I bring Amber with me?

-Cesar-yea yea sure, I haven't seen her in a long time, how is she?

-Me-she's doing well, I guess it's not a casual dinner then?

-Cesar-Na man, dress to impress, and get a sample of the greens you got ok, I'll send you the location, see you in a couple of hours, peace homz.

-Me-cool peace bro.

I called Amber and told her about the dinner invite at Cesar's place.

-Me- hey blonde how you doing, are you free later?

-Amber-hey babe, just closing up, yea what's up?

-Me-got invited to a formal dinner at Cesar's new place would like to come?

-Amber-sounds good, what do I have to wear?

-Me-the man said dress to impress Hun so let's look good tonight.

-Amber-ok, how much time do I have?

-Me- a couple of hours, and I'll come pick you up ok.

-Amber-just about enough time for me to get ready babe.

-Me-alright then see you in a couple of hours, say hi to your mom for me, peace.

-Amber-bye babe.

it's been a long time since I wore a suit, I barely have time to get ready, I had some of the greens here at the workshop hidden upstairs, I closed whatever I was doing, grabbed the greens and went straight home, I told mom that I'm having dinner at a friend's place tonight, went to my room,shaved my head and beard, hit the shower, got dressed in a black Italian suit, came out looking like new money, all that in under 90 minutes, god it's good to be a man, last detail was Darrell's Italian sport convertible coupe to match the suit, I mean how many kids you know at his age drives a car like this to college, my baby bro got good taste in cars .

I drove down to Amber's place, I rang the bell and she opened the door, I felt like I was picking her up for prom night, she looked like a James bond chic just stunning, I never seen her in an elegant dark red dress and high heels before and I don't think she ever saw me in a suit before, we both just stood there looking at each other for a while, I don't know what was going in her head but there was fireworks going on in mine, until her mom came to say hi and saw us, she broke the silence when she said

-Mrs. Peril-you better have her home by 12 you hear me DJ .
We just laughed for a minute and I said

-Me-sure thing Mrs. Peril.
-Mrs. Peril-you're a good man DJ, my baby talks about you all the time.
-Me-oh yea, what does she say?
-Amber-mom!

Amber just became a teenager at that second, she was actually blushing!

-Mrs. peril- ok fine, I'll tell you later DJ, take care you two.
-Me-good night Mrs. Peril.

I gently held her hand as we walked to the car,I opened the door for her and she got in the car then i closed the door and went to the driver's side, I looked up and saw her mom looking out of the window at us, with that I'm looking at my future son in law look in her eyes, we got on the way to Cesar's place, we didn't talk much, just enjoyed the music with the top down cruising in the nights cool breeze, in my mind I was thinking the hunt for the surgeon has begun, I'm visualizing what's going to go down at Cesar's place, I had a strong feeling that a deal was going to happen tonight with this guest who ever he might be, and that's why Cesar asked me to bring a sample, so I went on imagining what will go down and see it going the way I would like it to be and get the deal that I want for what I have .

we got to the address that Cesar sent me, I was surprised, the place was huge, we went through the main gate on a long drive way to the main house, passing through a huge garden, I felt like I was driving through central park, the main villa was a work of art with a fountain in front of the main door, I didn't believe that this was his place, we handed the car to the valet and Cesar came to meet us at the door.

-Me-I know I should have asked for a percentage when I handed you Kevin's business.

-Cesar-ha ha but you didn't, welcome to mi casa homz, oh my goodness Amber is that really you?

Cesar was surprised coz he remembers Amber as a simple young down to earth casual girl he shook her hand and didn't let go, Amber was smiling and said

-Amber-it's good to see you too Cesar, nice place, what have you been up too?

Cesar went into Spanish mood for a minute and I was just standing there not knowing what the hell he was saying, I snapped my finger in front of his face then I said

-Me-yo, C snap out of it man.

it took him a second to snap out of the tele Mondo mood but he did, after the warm welcome we had from Cesar at the front door, he said the other guests are not here yet and he had some time for a short tour of the new mansion which by the way was nothing short of amazing,a swimming pool with a retractable sun roof,a huge garden with lots of trees it's like he had his own little forest, big garage for his collection of expensive exotic cars, as we kept on walking and found ourselves behind the main house where the party is, leave it to Cesar to create a crazy exotic party with a Moroccan theme in every detail, a small band that's playing Arabic music with simple instruments, a tabla, an oud, a tambourine and a violin, which was enjoyed by many of the people in the party that night, it was a kind of a dreamy atmosphere going on, we were served Moroccan tea and ready rolled joints as we sat in an open tent overlooking a pond that had coy fish swimming in it, then he said ..

-Cesar-I have more surprises for you homz.
-Me-more than all this, what could you possibly have left?
-Cesar-just wait and you will see, just so you know this party is your welcome home party after jail, before you say anything I know it's a bit late but I was up to my ears in work, setting up what you gave me, it wasn't easy but I got it done, and this is the result of all that hard work .
-Me-wow this is too much bro, I don't know what to say...

-Cesar-you don't have to say anything, we are street brothers, you gave me a great gift DJ, and I wouldn't know how to repay you.

he was about to say more but his phone rang and he excused himself coz his other guest arrived and he will be back shortly, I turned to Amber, she was quite for too long and she had a look in her eyes that I knew very well ..

-Me-a joint for your thoughts...

-Amber-did you understand anything of what Cesar said to me when we arrived ?

-Me-not much, wait since when do you speak Spanish?

-Amber-I learned some in school and the rest from Cesar and the guys here before I met you.

-Me-ok, what did he say?

-Amber-he was surprised to see me, and apologized for not staying in touch for so long, he also asked me how can he make it up to me and his door is always open for me at any time .

-Me-Cesar still the same old latino charmer, I knew he was up to something when he kissed your hand, so are you going to take his offer or what?

-Amber-I might be nice but I'm not stupid, I'm not looking for the easy life anymore, not going to be a house pet for someone like Cesar, I got money now, my mom is with me, we have a nice house, and a bakery that's doing great, I'm happy, besides in the good or bad days nobody makes me feel so good about myself like you do, Cesar won't know a thing about that.

-Me-I do that?

-Amber-yes you do babe, and I love every bit of it.

I couldn't help but smile as we looked into each other's eyes, I had a hunch that there was something else she wasn't telling me, she put her head on my shoulder and held my hand while we enjoyed the music for a few more minutes, Cesar came back with his guests, he introduced us to a Mr. Felix carter who looked like a cheap version of Antonio Banderas with a short pony tail wearing a dark suit, he looked like he was in his early 40's, and his assistant that looked like a lab technician carrying a medium silver suitcase his name was Gary, I thought it was full of money, after the introduction we all sat down, that's when Cesar went behind the fancy bar behind us

-Cesar-I will be your bar tender tonight, what you like to drink?

-Felix-Jinn and tonic please.

-Me-any fresh juice you got bro
-Amber-juice for me too please
-Gary-beer if you don't mind.

Again I looked at amber

-Me-no drink?
-Amber-I don't feel like drinking tonight.

And again that smile, she's hiding some but I just can't be sure what it is, I gave her the woman what are you hiding look, and before I opened my mouth to say it Cesar brought the drinks and said

-Cesar-time for the main event, DJ you are going to love this.
-Me-love what?
-Cesar-this.

he clapped his hands and the lights went off for a few seconds and a small dance floor near the music band was lit and what you know a belly dancer appeared there, she was the center of attention of all who was there, she danced to the tunes of the band and enchanted the guests with her moves, she came close to where we sat and danced in front of us for a minute then went back to the stage at that time I imagined that I was a sultan sitting my palace and that dancer was dancing just for me, I was high so it really was like a 3D experience for me, the music stopped and the dance finished everybody was clapping for her as she left the stage,and I was sitting there with a big smile on my face, then I came back to the real world, I felt the side of my face was getting warm, I turned to find Amber staring at me like a jealous wife ..

-Me-what??
-Amber-you enjoyed that?
-Me-yea, Cesar did say this dinner party was for me so you know...
-Amber-did you know that I'm half Lebanese?
-Me-you are?
-Amber-yea, my mom is originally from there, she came to unnited states to study in college where she met my dad after and a short love story they

got married,a few years later she got the green card and a divorce when I was 5 and dad left since then, and still mom won't tell me why.
-Me-what does that have to do with me enjoying the dance?
-Amber-what I want to tell you is that I can dance like that, I learned from my mom, and that's why my step dad tried to rape me, I was a teenager then, he came into my room one day when I was practicing and my mom beat the hell out of him with a baseball bat, that's why mom went to jail.
-Me-ah, that explains your moms accent I thought it was an east European.
-Amber-no babe, I'll...
She was about to say something when Cesar said ..
-Cesar-hope you guys enjoyed the show, now let's talk business, DJ did you get the sample I asked for homz?
-Me-yea sure, there you go, best sativa money can buy.
he closed the tent, took the bag and gave it to Felix who opened the seal and smelled it then gave it to Gary, Gary opened the silver bag which turned out to be a miniature lab with test tubes and the whole works, he started examining the weed, he took a bud out smelled it then put it in a device that squeezed it hard got all of its juice into a tube, he looked at the color of the liquid, then got another tube with a transparent liquid in it and mixed it with the sativa juice, then said this will need about an hour to give us the result .

I was getting hungry, I asked Cesar when is dinner time and he said it should be ready by now, he opened the tent and the servants were getting the an arabian style dinner table set,an open air dinner under the stars, every 5 or 6 persons sat on large cushions and the food was surved on round tables for every groupe, I thought we were in an old James bond movie, on our way to the food table I was looking for roger moor among the guests, we sat down at the table and the servants brought the food, Cesar made a toast to me before we started to eat about our friendship and how I changed his life .

from the starters to the main course to the desert it was all arabic food, I'm talking grilled lamb or pigeons and quails, saffron rice, meat and chicken Moroccan tajins and other stuff that I simply don't know the names of, for desert the was kunafa, baklava and two or more things plus fresh fruits, there was a desert called Um ali meaning ali's mom made from milk topped with pistachio, funny name but real sweet and tasty, it was a real arabian feast, we enjoyed our meal and went back to the tent to chill and continue our business, the servants brought us Moroccan tea and arabic coffee, when I asked Cesar about how did he manage to do all that, he said it's a catering service that did all this, but you have to book them a week before your event ..

back to business, Gary took out the mix,checked the color and texture, and whispered to Felix saying (this the best sample we found so far), Felix didn't talk much since he came in, he asked Cesar about how much of this does he have, and Cesar told him that he should talk to me, his attitude changed and started to act a bit superior acting like he has other options, I thought it was business phycology and I went with it..

-Felix-Mr. DJ

-Me-yes sir.

-Felix-let's talk business, how much of this do you have and name your price.

-Me- to make a long story short, a little bird told me that you are producing a new drug and you need all the sativa you can get and I have it, I don't want cash I want to become a partner, I'm not talking about distribution like you offered Cesar no I'm looking at production partner .

The look on his face was priceless, and then he smiled and said

-Felix-we are not taking any partners on this project.

-Me-then you're not getting what you came here for.

-Felix-meaning?

-Me-if I don't get what I want, you won't either,

-Felix-and what makes you so sure that we can't get this from others.

-me-coz I made my deal with the few major growers who grow this pure strand, and let me assure you that I gave them the best deal they will get from any one for the next 2 years at least, it might take you 4 to 8 months or a year maybe to grow your own supply but it would also mean a great amount of delay on your plans to launch your product.

-Felix-I will offer you this for the last time, name your price

-me-no less than 45% partnership or nothing at all, I can make my money on the streets selling this stuff then later you can go around buying this a pound at a time if you like, think about it .

-Felix-Mr. Cesar you need to talk to your friend

Cesar approached me and whispered in my ear...

-Cesar- what are you doing DJ, take the money and maybe you can set up a deal with them as a supplier later.

-me-Cesar let me handle this, I see something in this deal that you don't, I have them where I want them just let it ride bro, watch me in action .

The time was getting late and I was ready to leave the party anyway...

-me-I'm not going to change my mind Mr. Felix, you have 72 hours to give me an answer or I'm going to start selling, I already have buyers waiting, it's was a pleasure to meet you and Mr. Gary too, Cesar I can't thank you enough for this great night, we really had a great time .

-Felix-the pleasure was all mines Mr.DJ

-Me-good night every one.

-Cesar-let me walk you out.

we left Mr. Felix and Gary in the tent and headed out with Cesar, we went through the main house to get to the main entrance, the three of us stood outside while we waited for the valet to bring the car, a minute later a dark green with a tan interior Bentley coupe parked in front of us and the valet brought the key to me, I told him this not my car, Cesar said DJ this is my gift to you, my tongue was tied and ambers eyes were glowing, she grabbed the key and went to check out the car .

-Me-this is too much bro I can't accept this car.

-Cesar-this is nothing bro, although you didn't ask for a percentage I save it for you but I couldn't get it into your bank account homz.

-Me-seriously.

-Cesar- yea man we have to find a way coz it's a lot of dineros, now were even brother, but I still can't understand why you want to become a partner with Felix on that new thing.

-Me-I will tell you later I promise bro.

I couldn't believe my ears, I was over the moon, I felt like I have finally accomplished what I have been working for all these years, and this guy handed it to me just like that, it was an emotional moment for us we shook hands and a bro hug, amber was in the car checking every detail .

-Me-alright bro I still need the other car, it belongs to Darrell he'll freak out if I don't bring it back home.

-Cesar-yea sure, it's parked down there here's the keys, how is he doing now?

-me-he left the hospital a few days after you came, and he's doing great, I can't thank you enough bro, words can't explain what I feel right now, good night bro .

-Cesar- love you brother, be safe, good night amber..

Amber was in another world at the time, she didn't even hear Cesar saying good night to her, Cesar went back inside and I went to amber who looked like a kid in a candy store .

-Me-amber, amber!!

-Amber-oh hey babe this car is amazing, luxury just feels so good.

-Me-so you like it.

-Amber-are you kidding I adore it.

-Me-good coz you going to have to drive it home, keep it for a couple of days .

-Amber-really?? Oh thank you thank you, I promise I'll be really careful Hun.

-Me-that's good to know, just be careful and keep your eyes on the road .

I showed her a few things about how deal with the car, and connected her phone to the cars audio system, sealed it with a kiss for good luck then both of us went on our way, that car looked like it was made for her, we were cursing together talking on speaker phone about the party and the how the car handles tell each of us got to his house and called it night.

2 days later I got a call from Cesar at around mid-day asking me to come over pronto, I dropped what I was doing at the workshop, took a shower, got into some clean clothes and hit the road, I got to Cesar's place, I called him to see where he was, and he told me to park the car and come inside the main house, I went inside and he was there alone, chilling on the veranda having a cold drink..

-Me-hey amigo, wzp?

-Cesar-couldn't be better brother, what about you?

-Me-doing great bro, so what's up, why the rush.

-Cesar- wanted to talk to you before Felix and his boss get here.

Felix and his boss wow, that had saved me a lot of time and effort to get to him, my plan is moving at full speed now, I need to be on my tows in the next chapter of this plan which is gaining their trust and not showing weakness .

-Me-oh yea, what do you want to talk about?

-Cesar-listen to me bro, I don't trust this guy Felix and to make things worse his boss Mr. Dean Camron.

-Me- what do you know about these people?

-Cesar-not much bro, I never heard of this Dean guy before,the first time Felix showed up at my place, all I know is that he's not a dealer like us, he's a business man from up north, owns a big pharmaceutical company, they've been asking around about you homz, and now Mr. Dean wants to meet you after what went down at the party, it seems like Mr. Felix is nothing more than a secretary, you can't trust people like that.

-Me-don't sweat it bro I got this planed out.

-Cesar-I hope so, from what I heard about this Dean guy is he's all about his money,nothing else matters much to him, that's why it's bad news to partner with this kind of people, it's better to stay at the side line .

-Me-sweet just the kind of guy I'm looking for bro.

-Cesar-I don't know what you mean or what's going on in your head, here light this up, these guys are going to be here soon, let's chill before they get here .

-Me-yea man, you been off the streets for a long time now, you had enough street racing bro?

-Cesar-Na man just didn't have enough time on my hands, my car needs some work, got to get it up to higher standers, remind me to send it to your garage later.

-Me-I got you bro.

-Cesar-there is some unfinished business between us.

-Me-what is it bro.

-Cesar-your share of the money homz, you want it in cash, or check or what?

-Me-yea about that,do you remember Shawn, the owner of the green lantern.

-Cesar-yea his car was stolen a while ago and later the found it chopped behind your workshop.

-Me-how the hell did you know about all that, you know what don't tell me, we rebuilt his car recently and it's back better than ever, he's my bank man so I'll ask him to call you and you can get this done through him alright ?

-Cesar-sounds good to me.

It was almost lunch time when Mr. Dean and his entourage arrived, Mr. Dean, Felix and two bodyguards, Mr. Dean looked like a very cool dad, about mid 50's had a resemblance to Billy Zane with a mustache and a goatee, Cesar and I met them at the door, Felix did the formal introductions and we all went inside, Cesar suggested we talk after lunch, the table was set for us in the dining room, we sat at the table and started our meal, I was hungry after I smoked that rocket with Cesar, so you can imagine how happy I was when Cesar said we'll talk after lunch, we mostly talked about small stuff, hobbies,women, cars, sports, you know topical guys chit chat, after a great homemade meal the four of us went to the living room, everybody is having a drink of their choice I asked Cesar for tea, Mr. Dean looked at me and said ..

-Mr. Dean-you don't drink much do you.

-Me-I don't drink at all, I stick to my smoke and that's it.

-Mr. Dean-I guess that's why the call you the chocolate man huh?

-Me-you got it.

-Mr. Dean-chocolate is another name for what?

-Me- hash.

-Mr. Dean-I see what about marijuana?, does it have any other names?

-Me-there are a few, but we call it veggies on the phone, this is our code name here between our friends and customers.

-Mr. Dean-ok and how much do you want for the full amount of veggies that you have right now?

-Me-I thought Felix told you, but to be safe I'll tell you again, I want to be a 45% partner in this new venture .

-Mr. Dean-son you have to understand that we are not taking partners and 45% is a very high percentage to ask for, it would be better for you to take the cash and enjoy it.

-Me-if I want the money, I know where to find it, but I'm looking for a bigger game, I heard that this new drug is the future, and I want to be a part of it.

Mr. Dean went quite for minute just looking at me, who knows what this old fox is thinking about, he took his jacket off, rolled up his sleeves, took another sip of his drink then said...

-Mr. Dean-let's smoke, do you have some of that sativa on you?

he surprised me and Cesar, he kept a poker face since he came in, none of us saw that coming,Cesar and I started looking at each other then we looked back at him and he said ..

-Mr. Dean-I went to collage to study pharmaceuticals, you can't imagine half of the things we did at that time, so come on let's light it up.

Cesar said that he had some left from the other night and went to get it, while I sat there with a smile on my face, Cease came back with the bag Mr. Dean opened it, and smelled it, took some of it then passed it to me and said...

-Mr. Dean-it's been too long since I rolled one of these,my rolling skills might be a bit rusty but I'm going to give it a try.

-Me- be our guest man.

He rolled a nice one, and started to smoke it then passed it to Cesar, he coughed a few times, and then he laid back and said

-Mr. Dean-that stuff is grade A quality.

-Me-we deal with only the best stuff Mr. Dean.

We smoked a couple, had a few laughs, then he said

-Mr. Dean-DJ my partners are not the easiest partners to deal with, the fact that you did your homework and you're using what you have as leverage to bargain your way into our world reminds me of my younger self, would you guys like to know a little secret ?

-Me-sure.

-Mr. Dean-I never graduated from college.

-Me-what?!, get the hell out of here.

-Mr. Dean-I was a damn good chemist too, I came up with a formula for a medicine and I was approached by a pharmaceutical company and I did the same thing you did to get a partnership deal and here I am today, DJ you need to lower your standers 45% is way too much to ask for.

-Me-what do you suggest?

-mr.dean-10%

-Me-I'm starting to like you Mr. Dean don't make me change my mind.

-mr.dean-10% of this can make you a very wealthy man in the near future DJ, take it

-Me-I can do 35%.

-Mr. Dean- 15%

-Me- 30%

-Mr. Dean- last offer 20% and you get the distribution rights if Cesar doesn't want it.

-Me-what do you think C?

-Cesar-my hands are full as it is, I guess you should take it.

-Me-Mr. Dean you got yourself a deal.

we shook hands on it and it was done, I finally got what I want,I'm one step closer to the surgeon, unfortunately I'm starting to like the old man, and since he said let's smoke Cesar was looking at him like the uncle he never had .

-Mr. Dean-great Felix will bring some papers for you to sign in a few days, excuse me but I need to use the gentlemen's room if you don't mind Cesar .

-Cesar- sure no problem.

Cesar escorted him to the toilet and Felix followed them, I sat in the living room then a remembered something that I wanted to talk to Cesar about, so I got up to look for him, I just want to say that when god is on your side he opens your eyes and ears to things you thought you will never know, I passed by the toilet and overheard Mr. Dean talking to Felix while he was washing his hands and Felix was holding the towel for him.

-Felix-are you sure about this agreement sir, I mean 20 % partner is a huge number of shares,what if he sells these shares to one of our competitors?

-Mr. Dean-keep your voice down Felix and listen, we just need to get our hands on the things we need then DJ might have an unfortunate accident shortly after he signs the papers, this deal will never see the light of day if I can do something about it, you disappointed me Felix, I thought you can handle a bunch of kids, not come crawling back with your tail between your legs, that's why you're still where you are.

After I heard that, in my mind I was saying thank you Mr. Dean, you just made my job easier, I think smoking that stuff lowered his guards down a bit, which was more than enough for me, he should have kept his mouth shut until he left this place, I thought I heard all I needed to hear so I slowly and quietly went back to the living room, when Mr. Dean came out and saw me smiling, he said.

-Mr. Dean- you have all the rights in the world to smile DJ you're about to become a very wealthy man.

-Me-I feel good and I just can't hide it, we need to celebrate this deal, please let us know as soon as possible when would be free to have some fun, I'll take you back to the old school days .

-Mr. Dean-sounds great, Felix will get back to you on that, remember DJ we want to get our hands on the veggies as soon as possible, it was pleasure to meet you son, it's always good to pump new blood to motivate a business .

-Me-the pleasure is all mine sir, have a safe trip home.

Cesar came back and we walked Mr. Dean to the door, he got into his car with Felix and his bodyguards and drove away, it was almost sunset, time for me to head back, I went back inside to use the bathroom and pick up my stuff, then Cesar walked me out to my car, I didn't tell him about what I heard Mr. Dean tell felix, I kept it to myself but I told him about the celebration plan and he suggested we do it on his new yacht, Cesar has a yacht !!, this guy is full surprises, any way I got in my car and drove back to my workshop to check on thing and close the shop down after everyone leaves and go home .

on the way back I was trying to come up with a plan to get as much information out of dean as soon as possible, and delay his plans of getting rid of me, it wasn't going to be easy, but I knew one thing for sure, I'm not going to give them anything until I come up with a plan, so if they want what I got they will have to wait for it, I need to plan two steps ahead if I want to bring these people down, I don't know how far I'm going to go with this yet but I'll finish it no matter what, I need to find Ruby and Atlas, I sent a message to Ruby before I went to bed asking her to contact me when she gets this message .

Next morning I called Cesar as he was having his continental breakfast and asked him if I can see his boat, he got mad when I said boat, he freaked out...
-Cesar-what do you mean boat I just gave you a Bentley and you call my yacht a boat homz, meet at me at the marina in two hours, I'll teach you the deference between a yacht and a boat you over roasted coffee bean .
-Me-what did you just call me ... hello hello!
Damn it he called me an over roasted coffee bean!! and hung up, left me hanging with my mouth open looking at the phone, basically it happened so fast and I didn't expect his reaction, to say the truth I didn't have a good come back to what he said, that means 1 point for Cesar 0 for me .
I had my breakfast,then went down to the workshop to start the work day, I went by Amber's bakery to get some snacks, usually Amber or her mom would be at the bakery, but today they were not there, then I headed out to the marina
I called Amber to see what's up, she said that she and her mom are at the hospital getting some medical tests done nothing to worry about and she was happy that I called, I'm puzzled, I know there is something she's hiding, I'm not going to ask instead I'm going to wait until she just say it .
I got to the marina and found Cesar standing there next to his car with his girls and the driver waiting for me, Cesar has an entourage now, I'm not sure what did I miss when I went to jail but hey I'm not complaining, I got out of the car and walked up to him, with that you called me an over roasted coffee bean look in my eyes and a food basket in my hand
-Me-good morning ladies and gentlemen.

-Cesar-oh you brought a picnic basket.

-Me-yes I did.

-Cesar-you don't need that where we are going, Alfredo please take the basket,DJ come with me homz.

-Me-are you sure that we don't need it?

-Cesar-DJ don't make me blindfold you, come on let me show you my boat.

we got in a golf cart and drove all the way to where the big yachts are, and along the way we passed by all kinds of boats, sail boats, speed boats you name it, we got to where the big boys park there yachts, now we are talking about floating villas, we got out of the golf cart and Cesar was explaining to me what I'm looking at and what kind of options I might find on them like a sales man, finally we got to a yacht with a sailor standing next to its entrance, when we came close he said ..

-Sailor-good day Mr. Lopez, we are ready to set sail, any special destination today sir.

-Cesar-hello martin, please ask the captain to just cruise the city coast line thank you.

then he turned to me and said welcome aboard the Diego, then he went in and the girls followed him and I was standing there, trying to get my head around what I'm looking at, it's a few feet short of a cruise ship, looking at how big it is on the outside is just awesome, good thing I had my shades on, otherwise he would have seen how my eyes popped, Cesar has become like one of those criminals in the James bond movies, I got on board and the inside blew me away,as we left the marina Cesar took me on a tour of the yacht and showed me the cabins, he had servants and a chef, the yacht had multiple decks, the decoration looked like Armani design, a helicopter landing pad on top, and a speed boat in a garage in the lower deck, we took some time to enjoy the trip over a cold drink and a smoke .

suddenly a plan jumped in my mind, I sat down with Cesar on the main decks living room looking out at the city, and told him about what happened at his villa with Mr. Dean and what I heard him say to Felix, I told him that I want to kidnap Mr. Dean and stop the production of this new drug, coz I had my own reasons and if this drug goes out on the street it's going to seriously affect his business in the near future, I still kept ruby, atlas and the aliens details from him, I just told him what he needs to know which is more than enough for him,

He was very quiet throughout the time I was talking ...

-Me-so are you with me?

-Cesar-again you look after me without me even knowing, I'm in let's make it happen, what do you need me to do ?

-Me-first let's head home, second open your ears and listen carefully.

I gave him all the plan details so he can be ready when it goes down, we got back to the marina, I had fun on that short cruise with Cesar and the girls, it gave me a taste of luxury life at its best, now it's time to head back to the workshop finish a few things and head home to chill and finalize the fine details of my plan, I knew I needed a foxy lady in this plan, I got to find a vixen or a cogar to make it complete .

The days passed by so slow while we waited for Felix to call, finally the call came, and we had a couple of days to get ready for the party, everything was ready all we had to do is bring it all together, and finally it's on, the night party on the yacht was a blast, I played some old school hits for Mr. Dean and his friends, then my plan went into play mood, I had a simple and smooth plan,to get Mr. Dean away from his bodyguards and Felix, that's where are vixen Monica comes in, the plan went in effect a couple of hours into the party, Monica stepped into the picture making eye contact with Mr. Dean while she is sitting at the bar, he offers her a drink, then she took him out on the dance floor, things got hotter so she lured Mr. Dean into going to one of the cabins for some fun, he told his boys that he will be back in an hour or so, in the cabin she fixed him a drink and put a couple of drops of sleeping potion in it

then she starts to do a dance while she takes her clothes off taking her time until the sleeping potion takes effect, when Mr. Dean fell asleep, Monica left the cabin after turning off the lights and locking the door, she sent me a message saying it's done, then 15 - 20 minutes later she started to scream for help, we dropped a Wight overbred to make a splash sound,by the time Mr. Deans bodyguards rush to her, they found her hanging for her life from the side of the yacht,when they pulled her up she told them that Mr. Dean fell overbred as they were kissing after they left the cabin and they tripped over the side, the party stopped, and the emergency lights were lit on the side of the yacht to try to find Mr. Deans body, but he was nowhere to be found, so our best guess was is that he was dragged under the yacht because of the propeller suction and drowned .

Cesar told the captain to turn the yacht around and head back home, the police and the coast guards were notified of the accident, the police was waiting for us when we arrived and the coast guards were already out there looking for deans body, we had wrapped Mr. Dean in one of the bed sheets and got him off the yacht when the police came on board to investigate, we snuk him out of the cabin in a box with the DJ's equipment, after everybody left and the coast was clear we took Mr. Dean out of the box and into the trunk of my Bentley, I didn't get a reply from ruby since I sent her a message the other day so I thought I'll take my chances and go to the naval base where I met atlas for the first time, and maybe I'll get lucky and find him there, I drove all the way there, came to the front gate and got out of the car and stood there, it was dark and no one was at the security both at the gate and lights at all, I looked up at the camera and said, (I know you can see and hear me, I want to speak with atlas now it's extremely urgent, tell atlas that DJ is outside and I have a surprise for him) .

now I don't have a clue if these people are still working here or if they had left the place, I got back in my car and sat there waiting for something to happen, I waited for about 2 minutes then I thought that they must have left this place, and just when I was about to drive away the light at the gate was lit and the gate opened, I opened the car window and drove slowly towards the gate, when I was passing through the gate I heard a sound coming from the security both telling me to drive towards the next light I see inside, I looked to the front and saw one of the pear lights turned on, I kept on driving until I got there, I stopped there then an arrow lit up directing me to go to the right, on my right was a huge warehouse and the pear was on my left .

the warehouse door rolled open and I drove inside, still I'm driving in total darkness only using my cars head lights, a few feet inside and I heard the warehouse door closing behind me, I thought I saw someone coming towards me from my left side, I turned off the engine and got out of the car and when the warehouse door was completely shut the lights tuned on and I saw that it was atlas walking and two other guys, when he got closer he said..

-Atlas-good to see you again DJ, it's been a while since the last time we met.
-Me-it's good to be seen, how you been?

-Atlas-ooh busy with work as usual.

-Me-and what about Ruby what is she up to, haven't heard from her since the last time you guys came together.

-Atlas-she ok, she's working undercover, trying to get some info for the past few weeks.

-Me- are you sure she's ok?

-Atlas-yea yea sure she stays in contact, she calls once a week to keep us updated on what she finds, and so far it's not much .

-Me-I thing you should get her out of there.

-atlas-yea I think so too, so you got me a Bentley very nice, my favorite color too, I got to say I like it .

-Me-sorry to disappoint you but it's not the car; it's what's in the trunk.

-Atlas-and what's in the trunk?

-Me-this guy.

I opened the trunk and uncovered Mr. Dean sleeping like a baby, and atlas was surprised to see him in there...

-atlas-that's Dean Camron, the owner of meds Inc., we have been watching this guy for the past year, we thought he might have some connection with the production of Slip Dream but we couldn't come close enough to him coz he's very well connected to politicians, how did he get in your trunk ??

-Me-first help me get him inside and I'll tell you the story later.

atlas asked his guys to help us take him inside and they brought a small cargo trolley, we stuffed dean in it and took him inside to a room where he spent the rest of the night sleeping, I sat with atlas and told him how all this came to be, then later I left the base and went home, and left things in atlas hand to see what kind of info he can get out of Mr. Dean.

the next morning Mr. Dean woke up on a white hospital bed in a strange place, surrounded by 4 white walls, a thick steel door, ac ventilation a TV with a camera next to it, some food and water on a table nearby, a bidet and a sink, I don't know if you can imagine how he must have felt when he woke up, I mean from where he was last night to this place, he must have thought he's in a weird dream or something, it took him a while to see that this is all true, he got up did what he had to do, washed his face and sat down to eat, he was watching TV when he saw the news about him drowning last night and the coast guard couldn't find his body and he was announced dead to the world, that shocked him to the core of his soul, he was left in the room with no contact from any one, leaving him to think and think some more while they watched him from the other room .

Atlas sent word to ruby to quit whatever she was doing and come back, coz there was no need to for her to stay there any longer, and she did just that, two days after this incident Cesar called me up to see if everything is ok and told me that he has another buyer for the weed he said his name was solo, and he wants it fast, and he also said that money is no problem, I told Cesar to give me his number, I'll deal with this from now on, atlas left Mr. Dean just the way he is for 3 days no contact from anyone, he started to freak out and scream at the camera, he reached the point of breaking down, he was almost out of food and water,and on the fourth day Mr. Dean didn't bother to get out of bed, all he did was watch TV and nothing else, atlas called me and asked me to come after 8 pm to the base coz they will interrogate Mr. Dean tonight and he wanted me to be there and I wasn't about to miss the show, I closed my workshop an hour early and hit the road.

I got there and atlas said that they are about to start, I sat there to watch atlas in action on the monitor screen, atlas went into the room with 2 guys, as soon as the door opened dean got up and started yelling at them, atlas stood there like a block of ice just staring at dean,and the guys stod there just in case Dean might do something crazy, atlas waited until dean burned his energy out, then looked him straight in his eyes and said..
-Atlas-you're a dead man dean, to me, to your family and to the rest of the outside world, and that makes you mine, I can do whatever I want to do with you and only god can judge me .
-Dean-who the hell are you, where am I, and what do you want from me?
-Atlas-my name is not of your concern, and you are where I want you to be, and what I want from you is information about the new drug your company is working on, and who are your partners .
-Dean-and what if I don't cooperate?
-Atlas-oh there won't be any physical harm done to you, I'll just leave you here for a while and come back later coz it looks like you're starting to like this place, tell me what I want and I'll put you in a place where you can see the sun and talk to people, think about it and I will come back later.

dean agreed to what atlas told him before Atlas even got up from his chair, then he started to spill out everything, I got to say I liked the way Atlas did this, he was very smooth for a big guy, I sat there and heard all that dean said about the drug the labs and finally Patrick Solomon aka the surgeon the brains behind it all, when atlas asked him about where can we find the surgeon, he said that he's probably looking for a supplier right now since I couldn't supply the weed, the man is rich and likes to have fun, loves stuff that gives him an adrenaline rush and most of all he loves cars, he loves to race for high stakes, when Dean said those words I knew just what to do to find the surgeon, atlas came out of the room and came to me and asked me ...

-Atlas-you heard what the man said, what are going to do about it?

-Me-I think I have a plan, a friend of mine told me that he has another buyer his name is solo, I'm thinking that he might be the surgeon, I'm going to try to make him come here to set up a deal .

-Atlas-if you think that's it's him then you going to need my help on this next phase, he's no easy prey like dean.

-Me-at least show me how he looks like.

-Atlas-come with me, I think we still have his file in the system.

we went to his office, atlas sat behind his desk and started looking through the files on his computer, then he turned the computer screen my way and I saw the surgeons face, it was like looking at a picture of a puma, an ambush predator, you can see it in his eyes, plus he's an electronics expert, amazing background in combat training and tactics expert, it was a long list to go through, in short an almost perfect combat machine, the question that went through my mind was how to bring this guy down in the fastest way possible ..

-Me-are you sure that this guy is human??

-Atlas- he can smell an ambush a mile away and almost predict your next move, that means that you have to be real careful DJ .

-Me-the question is do you think that he still looks the same or might have done something to change his looks?

-Atlas-we have only one way to find out.

-Me-how?

-Atlas- retinal scanning, I can provide you with a contact lenses that can do that, if you can get him to look you straight in the eye we can get a positive ID, and an ear piece so you can hear me .

-Me-sounds good to me, just let me know that it's him and leave the rest to me.

-Atlas-do you have a plan?

-Me-not yet, but it will come to me when the time is right.

-Atlas-then you have to take these.

-Me-still with the nanobots.

-Atlas-it's the only way that we can keep track of you and get the information we need, you can wear a wire but he will find out, besides taking these nanobots won't hurt in any way and we can take them out of you any time no pain no harm done, it just might take you a few days to get use to your new abilities, it's going to take a couple of hours to get them in your body, come on DJ you just saw how big this guy is, if you get in a fight with him you have to be on top of your game, and he's military trained too, which makes him a more experienced fighter than you are .

I was finally convinced to take the nanobots, so we went to an operating room complete with a medical staff waiting there, they asked me to take my clothes off and just keep my shorts on, I laid down on a bed and they started attaching monitors to my body from my head all the way down to my legs, they took readings of my bodies bio functions from the monitors and gave the all clear to start, an IV fluid was administered in my vain then they started to add the nanobots to it, there were six small containers of nanobots which they added one at a time, when I asked why atlas told me that it has to be done like that to be able to put every group of nanobots where it should go, all I felt was the cool fluid going into my blood stream, then some tingling in some parts of my body which meant that the bots are attaching to certain areas of my nervous system and muscles, atlas stayed with me throughout the whole operation talking to me, I heard one of the medical team say that all the bots are in place we are ready for the start phase, then atlas he said .

-Atlas-I'll see you in an hour.

-Me-are we done yet?

-Atlas-almost done, they will to put you to sleep to turn on the bots and be sure that everything is going the way it should, in other words a diagnostic check, don't worry you'll be just fine DJ, doctor you may proceed .

-Me-this is taking longer than you told me, I got work to...

The doctor already administered the sleeping potion in me and I fell asleep before I can finish my sentence, I woke up a little later all alone no wires attached to me accept one to monitor my heart beat, I pulled it off and put my clothes on, I heard someone talking outside the room then the door opened and atlas came in the room, with a cup of coffee in his hand.

-Atlas-hey champ, you feel good?
-Me-like a million dollars, best hour of sleep in a long time, is that coffee for me?
-Atlas-sure here you go but be careful.

as he was saying be careful he handed me the cup, I took the cup by the handle and it broke, the cup fell down and half way while it was falling a caught it with my other hand and not a single drop was lost, I was amazed, I looked like a kid who just got a new bike for Christmas, then I looked at Atlas and he laughed and clapped his hands...

-Me-that was crazy, I didn't mean to do that.
-atlas-ha ha, very nice, I know you would be a fast learner, now you just need to be a little more delicate in dealing with objects in your daily life, later I need you to come back here in a few days so we can run some more tests ok .
-Me-sure why not, now I got to go take care of some things.
-Atlas- let me walk you out.

on our way out he told me more about my new enhanced abilities and how I should take things easy and give my brain sufficient time to learn to coop with the new upgrades, he also showed me what's happening to people as we speak, the production of the drug might have been slowed down a bit but the aliens are still at it, they are using the amount they have and stealing people's lives as we speak, casualties are at the same rate and these guys are not thinking about stopping, that means we have to put a stop to this as soon as possible .

I left the base with one thing on my mind, how can you bring down a guy like the surgeon, I have the bait and nothing else, one word kept coming up in my mind (surprise), I have to catch him on our first meeting but how, I'll just have to make the call first and see what kind of feeling I get from the guy, then and only then will I come up with a plan to catch that cat.

I got in my ride very carefully, didn't want to risk damaging anything, I asked myself why waste time, I have the number I'll make the call and satisfy my curiosity, the phone was linked to the car so I said call solo, the phone rang a few times and finally a person with a very deep voice picked up, it seems whoever it was on the other end was using a voice changer to hide his true identity

-Solo-hello DJ, I'm glad that you finally decided to make the call.
-Me-I apologize if I kept you waiting Mr. Solo, but I have been a bit busy, surely you understand.
-Solo-never mind the waiting, what's important is that you did, we can talk freely this is a secure line, name your price let's end this here and now.
-Me-I want a partnership like I told Mr. Dean and he agreed to 20% plus distribution rights but we didn't get to sign any papers before his unfortunate accident.
-Solo-dean was never going to make that deal, and nether will I, so name your price.
-Me- Mr. Solo it's not that easy, you know and I know that you don't have much of a choice in this, if you had found what you were looking for out there you wouldn't be wasting your time talking to me.
-Solo-this game is too big for a kid like you.
Oh no he did not just call me kid! I took a deep breath and kept my cool
-Me-I'm willing to move up to the next level and I'm a fast learner, I heard that you're a gambling man, race me for it .
-Solo-and what's the catch?
-Me-I win I get my deal 20% partner and supplier plus distribution, you win I give it to you for free, all or nothing are you up for it.
The guy went quite for a few seconds, was he suspicious or what, whatever it is I have to nudge him out of his comfort zone pronto...

-Me-what.... is this game too big for you, using a voice changer is one thing but backing up from a challenge is another, I thought you had bigger balls than that, am I talking to the man in charge or are you just another Felix, come on its just me and you, man to man winner takes all what do you say boy?
I think I pushed the right button when I said Felix or boy or maybe both I don't know coz he removed the sound changer and said...
-Solo-alright you got your wish, name the time and place.

-Me-whenever you're ready get your ass down here, I'll be waiting with a pen and a contract for you to sign that says that we are partners, and you better bring your A game coz I don't like easy wins .

I hung up, there was nothing more to be said, I hope he takes the bait, all I need of him is to show up and the rest will be history, all I know right now is that I need to get some shut eye, I got to do some work on my ride tomorrow so I got to be in top mental shape to do this, no mistakes, coz if I lose this race I'm out.

the next couple of days were stressful, having to be extremely careful with everything is just not easy, from breaking nuts and bolts to bending door handles and cracking my phone screen and bending forks and spoons and other crazy stuff, it's almost a nightmare to roll a blunt, the pipe saved my life until I got my handle back on the skill of rolling again, I learned not to put on my jeans in a hurry the hard way, a combination of a wedge and a kick in the nuts at the same time, I almost fainted, it brought me down to my knees, day by day I made my peace with it and managed to put things back in order .

I also asked around about solo,did my homework, turns out that he has been terrorizing street racers with his baby bull, I mean a modified Lamborghini Gallardo, and if he thinks he can do this here, I got something up my sleeves waiting for him .

three days have past and I had to go back to Atlas for some test he want to make to be sure that everything is going well with my improvements, they gave me a body suit that monitors everything that goes on inside my body and send it to the control room, the man put me through all kinds of tests that you can imagine for stamina, strength, speed, physical reflexes from morning until noon, then I had a meal and took a nap for a few hours then the real fun started, Ruby came to wake me up, I was real happy to see her, I got up and we went to an observation room, which was as big as a football field, with a running track around it, there was a huge window on one side of the room, Atlas was on the other side of the glass, Ruby left me in there and went to the other side too, atlas spoke to me on the mic .

-Atlas-can you hear me DJ?

-Me-yes loud and clear, what am I doing here again, I thought we did it all this morning.

-atlas-no were not done yet, this morning we tested if your body has accepted the nanobots this is the part where we get to test how the bots work, Ruby will be your operator whatever you need just ask her and she will program it into you, remember how fast you ran this morning.
-Me-hell yea.
-Atlas-go ahead ask for speed.
-Me-ok, ruby hit me up with some speed.
-Ruby-you got it papi.
As soon as she hit send I felt a shiver like a cold chill for a second.
-Atlas-what are you waiting for run.

I put my foot down and took off full speed ahead, it felt so fast that I left my shadow behind, I took a couple of laps of the place in less than a minute and stopped where I started .

-Atlas-what do think about that?
-Me-very impressive man I love it.
-Atlas-good, coz you just ran half a mile in under 45 seconds.
-Me-wooow, that's what I'm talking about, and I wasn't really pushing it.
and more tests, I can jump higher and further than I could have ever imagined, bending steel with my bare hands became easy, better eye sight and hearing,faster reflexes, I'm almost superman, except that I'm not bullet proof and can't fly .
-Atlas-are we having fun DJ?
-Me-oooh yea T, I can do this all day, hell all year if you let me.
-Atlas-I'm afraid we're done for the day DJ, come back tomorrow for one more thing to rap all this up.
-Me-let's do it now, I got time.
-Atlas-do you even know what time is it DJ?
I looked at the clock on the wall and I remembered that I have to close up shop and pick up some things for my mom on my way back home, well I'll have to come back tomorrow, I checked my phone on my way out and found a message from solo that said he will be here in 72 hours or less and I should get ready, oh I'm ready all right, I think he took his time to get ready and done some research before coming here, it shows just how careful he is about details,I got to the workshop and checked everything out and closed it up, got my mom's things and went home .

next morning I woke up to find a message from Ruby that said (good morning papi you need to get here after 6 pm, it's going to be more fun than yesterday I promise xoxo), hmmm I like fun so I replied (will be there sweet cheeks), I had a big breakfast, went to the workshop and took care of business for the day and closed up an hour early, had a sandwich on my way to Atlas, today is weapons training, got my body suit on and got in the training room there was a few things added targets and mannequins, atlas and ruby were waiting for me in there, they were talking about something and ruby was carrying a small red box when I came closer to them they stopped .

-Me-what's up guys, did I interrupt anything?

-Atlas-hey DJ, nothing you should worry about.

-Me-how are you doing my smooth operator?

-Ruby-smooth as silk papi.

-Me-I like the sound of that, so what do we have today, are you going to give me a gun?

-Atlas-what I have for you makes guns a thing of the past, it's one of the reasons why the surgeon attacked our old headquarters, the person that created this was killed in that attack and we don't have any of the plans of how to make other ones, they all got burned in the attack, so what you're going to get is a one of a kind weapon, and you got to be real careful with it.

-Me-that bad ha?, what is it?

-Atlas-to tell you the truth DJ I'm not really sure I should hand it over to you.

-Me-don't worry atlas I promise I won't lose it, now show it to me.

he got me on edge for a moment, then he asked ruby to open the box and there were 4 rings, we were quite for a few seconds, I was expecting something else, I looked up to find atlas looking at me so I said ..

-Me-what..... Should I be impressed, or are you proposing to me?

-Atlas-what you see in front of you is a result of years of work and research by one of our top scientists who was killed in the attack, he made only six rings gathered from what we have collected over the years from alien wrecks, he was able to understand and put together a few weapons from alien technology, some were damaged beyond repair in the attack, these rings work with the nanobots that are in certain areas of your brain, you can wear them all in one hand or 2 in each hand, and whatever weapon you can imagen will be in your hands instantly in laser forum, don't let your imagination limit you .

-Me-you said six I see only four.

-Atlas-Solomon has 2.

-Me-right, ok, I see where this is going.

-Atlas-you need at least two rings for them to work,they are adjustable and from mater that's bio-metallic that's out of this world they will fit your size, one ring just won't do, put them on and Ruby will start the programing process in a minute and we will see how you can handle this, be real careful DJ, this is no joke make sure you hurt the other guy not yourself.

then he turned around and left me standing there with Ruby, I put 2 in each hand, then ruby closed the box, kissed me, wished me good luck and went behind Atlas, they went into the control room and Ruby started tapping away on the computer, I started to warm up, moving my hands and legs trying to get ready for the test, I looked at the control room and every one in there was looking at me like I'm going to suddenly transform or fly, any way they all had that high expectations look in their eyes at that moment in time, I waved at them with a smile, Ruby looked at me and said we are ready if you are papi, I gave her the thumps up and atlas said ok DJ show me what you can do, first move I did was the wolverine claw, with the face and the stance and only two laser claws came out, one for each hand, I was amazed and disappointed at the same time .

-Me-what only 2?!

-Atlas-really DJ, ok try them out on the targets.

-Me-if you say so, ruby hit me up with some fighting skills.

-Ruby-anything in special papi?

-Me-chose your top 3 and hit me up, throw some speed in there too.

seconds later and I felt that light shiver in my body, and I went buck wild on the targets slashing and cutting like crazy while jumping, twisting, and flipping through the air and jumping of the walls, it's crazy how these rings work, I just think of a weapon and it's in my hands in a blink of an eye, I tried laser sword, double blades, big guns, machine guns, whips, ninja stars and more, whatever came to my mind I did it, I turned that play room into a junk yard, all targets were eliminated, I didn't hear anything from Atlas or Ruby for a few minutes, I looked at them and everyone in the room were just standing there watching, and Atlas was having some popcorn .

-Me-do you have any more targets for me, coz this was too much fun.

-Atlas-how do you feel DJ?

-me-I feel great, I can do this longer, it's strange I just feel a bit hungry, all throw I had a big meal before I came here .

-Atlas-I see, I guess you got the general idea about your new upgrades, that's enough for today come out take off your body suit and join us here.

-Me-come on T just a few more targets man.

-Atlas-you turned them all to dust DJ, come to my office, we need to talk.

I left the play room,i had a shower and put on my clothes and went to where atlas and ruby are, after all that I still couldn't get the smile off my face, I never had so much fun in my life, we sat down and atlas gave me a chocolate bar and started asking me about how it felt throughout the workout, and if there was any updates with this solo guy, I told him everything that happened in the past few days, and my deal with solo, and it's about to go down in less than 48 hours, he asked me if I had a plan and I said not yet, let's see if he's the person we're looking for first then we'll see where we go from there .

I was getting ready to leave when atlas gave me a small box that had the contact lenses and the ear piece which looked like a capsule and a small magnet, atlas told me that it goes deeper than the usual ear pices inside the ear so it's not to be seen, and later if you want to remove it you use the magnet, Atlas also said that they have had some good luck, they raided some of the locations that Mr. Dean gave them, closed and arrested some of the people who worked on manufacturing slip Dream, thanks to me, I was over the moon with this bit of news, it made me feel like I was a part of something big, that was the end of my day with Atlas and Ruby .

I found a message on my phone from Amber asking if I was free for dinner, I replied with a yes if she would meet me at the workshop in 45 minutes, I got to the workshop and found Amber waiting outside,we went upstairs,she brought Italian food, it's like she read my mind, she looks like she had put on a few pounds, gained some healthy weight, but still it looked good on her if you know what I mean, we sat down for dinner, she started serving the food in plates and acting like this was a family dinner, I mean we don't usually do that, I didn't comment on any thing, but it shows in my eyes that I'm surprised, any way we had a great meal while watching TV, after that I said let's have a smoke but she said that she has to go, it's been a long day for her too, so I thought I'll save it for home, as she was leaving she kissed me and looked me in the eye and said .

-Amber-I know that there is something you're not telling me Hun, but I know you will when you're ready.

-Me-there's something you're hiding too, you been acting different since Cesar's party.

-Amber-you think so?

-Me-I know so babe, so are you going to tell me anytime soon?

-Amber-I'll tell you when you tell me.

suddenly it turned into a staring contest, we stood there staring into each other's eyes, I can't tell her what I'm working on with Ruby and Atlas, on the other hand I'm not really sure that I want to know what's on her mind .

-Me-you know what, maybe this not the right time, but I'll give you a hint, what I'm working on these days is because of what happened to Darrell back at the fest .

-Amber-fair enough, I will tell you this bit of extra weight is not because I'm just munching on my bakery products, and it's going to stay with me for some time weather you like it or not ok Hun.

-Me-you know what. I think I like it, it looks good on you.

-amber-I'm glad you do, I can see that you're happy to see me and I would love to spend the night, but you look like you need to get some rest Hun, and I do too, I came to see how you are doing, I just missed spending some time alone with you, promise me that whatever you're doing you will take care of your self ok .

-Me-don't worry I will.

we hugged kissed and she put her head on my shoulder for a minute, we just stood there in each other's arms, then we gathered our stuff and walked out to our cars, and we both went are separate way, I got home and had my joint and slept like a baby .

the next day I got an message from solo saying that he's in town and wants to know about our race details, I didn't reply I just left it until later in the day to make a decision about where would be the best place, it took me a while to come up with this race course but I finally sent him the course to view it on GPS and meet me at the starting line at 9.00 p.m., the course runs from the edge of the city with some twists and turns then on to the high way for a free speed run and ends at the ship docks for some more turns and drifts to finish in exit tunnel where only one car can pass, same place where I caught Kevin, an hour later he replies (let's meet,then we'll see about that course), I still had some time before race time so did some work at the shop then went home early for a good meal and a nice nap, yes I slept on it and I visualized the race in my mind and saw myself win .

finally it's time to hit the road to the starting point of the race, I called Ruby to make sure that we stay in contact all the time, got the contact lenses in one eye and the ear piece in place all are working well, they can see what I see and I can hear them perfectly, they can track where I am with the nanobots and hear me too, I wore the rings and put on racing gloves on to hide them, and I brought a small electric Taser just to be safe, I got to the place a little early, turned off my car to give time to cool down, I attached my laptop to the car to do some final system checkups while I wait for solo .

I was a bit on edge coz I felt that this solo guy was up to no good, it's been a long time since I felt like this before a race, I had a sample of the stuff with me so I disconnected the laptop and rolled a small one just to bring me down a bit, solo was late but he finally showed up and not alone,and I got to tell you this guy travels in style, he arrived with two guys, a mechanic and a technician in a luxury tour bus, one of those mobile homes, that has a parking space under it to fit a small sport car and a motor bike at the back of it .

-Me-Ruby are you there.
-Ruby-I hear you papi.
-Me-do you see what I see?
-Ruby-yes papi, it's a bit dark though.
-Me-is atlas there?
-Atlas-here DJ we are ready.
-Me-ok let's get this party started.

solos mechanic got the lambo out from the parking space under the bus and parked it at a distance as solo got out of the bus and walked towards me while his boys were doing some last minute checks on the car, there was a street light between us so I walked to it to meet him under the light, we got there and stood there sizing each other silently, like a western movie just before a shootout, I felt like I was looking at Kevin, he emits the same energy, acts like he can control his surroundings or know what's going to happen next, in my mind I was trying to remember the picture that atlas showed me of the surgeon when he was in his mid-20's, this guy looks the same when he should be 10 or 15 years older, then I heard atlas say ...

-Atlas-good god, it's him, the retinal scan is positive, it's like time stood still for this guy.

I decided to break the silence...

-Me-welcome to my town.

-Solo-thank you, I don't believe that you came alone.

-Me-should I be afraid of you or your two friends waiting back there?

-Solo-maybe you should consider the stakes riding on this race.

-Me-that's the beauty of it, let me ask you this, are you a man of your word?

-Solo-yes I am.

-Me-then we got nothing to worry about, we race and as we agreed the winner gets his prize, although I came alone but if you want to try anything remember your in my house, you won't leave this state in one piece and this goes for your boys too and you won't get what you came all the way here for, come on solo you're looking at your future partner now, we should be on the same page boy.

-Solo-don't be so sure nobody has passed this baby yet.

-Me-come on you should know that you can't catch a stallion with a steer man.

-Solo-I don't like the course you set for this race, I checked it out earlier today, it doesn't have much road for a top speed run.

-me-it has a bit of everything, I planned it with you in mind, this track will take your car and you to the limit, plus I already got people scouting the rout for police cars and to close some turns to give us a clear course .

-Solo-we should even the odds, we play follow the leader, whoever stays in front more than 30 seconds is the winner.

-Me-this is not a video game man, you can never be sure about the timing, why don't we flip a coin for it?

-Solo-ok call it.

I won the coin flip, I called Yoshi to start closing the entrances to the high way, a minute later I got an message saying we are clear to start, solo asked one of his guys to wait at the finish line he took the motor bike and left, the other one lined us up to start the race, then he started talking about his lambo's, horse power, upgrades, 0-60, I can tell he was trying to intimidate me with numbers and trying to get into my head with all that stuff, little does he know that I'm immune to bull shit, we shook hand and I walked back to my car .

-Me-guys can you hear me?
-Ruby-every word papi loud and clear.
-Me-I need to be fast on my reflexes hook me up girl.
-Ruby-you got it, good luck, show Atlas how you do it on the black top papi.
-Me-let's get this show on the road, Atlas if you can hear me don't blink.
as we got on the starting line I got into my race mode, I felt it, my zone, my race, I saw the rout from the begining all the way to the end, I almost forgot that solo was next to me revving his car and looking at me, trying to distract me, but he doesn't know how deep in concentration I was, when I came back to earth I looked at him and smiled, his face changed I think he felt my foot kicking his ass, I revved my engine a couple of times to get the oil flow going, burned some rubber to get better traction on my rear wheels, got to the line, I kept the gear on first with left foot on the clutch and right foot on the gas, revved the engine up to 4000 rpm and waited for a few seconds and when the light flashed I jumped the line like greased lightning .

I got the jump but he had the 4 wheel drive advantage on me so we went head to head until the first turn that's when the scale started to shift between us with every turn, this guy knows his car very well, that lambo can turn on dime, I have to break loose from this guy, I know these streets and he's driving like he was born on these streets, I haven't had a run like this in a long time, damn it feels good, now it's time for the free run on the high way, he caught on it seconds before I did and he just went into light speed mode, all I saw was the blue nitrous flames shooting out of his exhaust tips and boom he's gone, I don't know what the hell he had on that car all I know is that he is using everything for this part of the race, I guess he wanted to get as far away from me as he can so he can chill a bit when we get to the docks .

we had a clean run so far, I used one stage of my nitrous to catch up and stay close to solo, I can tell that his car was made for this part of the race,we were doing around 200 mph easy, I was doing my best to stay close, hiding behind him just using him to cut down the wind resistance otherwise he would just be too far to catch, by the time we get to the last leg of this race, I planned to use him as a catapult just before we get to the docks, right now I'm wishing that we get to the docks asap coz my car was heating up like crazy, all because I'm too close to his tail, all the hot air coming out of his exhaust is heating my engine coolers, but I don't have much of a choice, if I take my foot of the gas he might just be long gone, I love my car but I'm willing to burn this engine to win this race, I got so much riding on this race, I can't afford to lose .

I can tell that solo is on edge, coz I'm close enough to see him looking at me in his rear view mirror every few seconds, my guys did a great job of closing some of the entrances to the high way disguised as road maintenance crew, the street was just for solo and I, after we pass the guys would just move away to let the traffic flow back into the high way, I kept looking at the temperature gauge and has almost passed the yellow and going into the red zone, we were about a mile away from the docks so I gave him a bit of distance just to give my baby space to breath some cool air, we have a 360 degree exit to the docks and in there would be my last chance to end this race to my advantage .

I noticed that solo doesn't burn rubber on his turns, taking every turn just the right way on the entrance and exit, so I'm hoping that the docks would be a nightmare for him, when we go to the exit I shifted down gradually from 6th gear to 4th and he was still in front, and when we entered I waited for my chance, he was sticking to the inside corner of the exit and left so much space on the other side, and that's where I saw my chance to overtake him, I shifted down to 2rd gear and punched it hard, I managed to drift around him and take the lead, going into the docks, and that's where I got the upper hand, it was a race between containers, large machinery, and cement blocks to the exit on the other side, only one can pass, I did my magic, took my car to the absolute limit of its performance, I did my best to cut every turn at the right angle and this guy was still on my tail but I had a two car lead on him, I can see the exit straight ahead after the last turn, I lined up the car straight and punched my 2nd stage of nitrous to make my escape .

my tires were too hot after all the drifting, so when I hit the nitrous I didn't get all the traction I was hoping for, I lost some of that power burning rubber which brought solo even closer to me, he was almost next my rear left tire when he nudged me to the right as I was entering the exit tunnel, he knew that he lost the race so he did that and slowed down to watch me crash, I drifted to the right at an angle, I turned the steering full right just enough to get the car in the exit and not to crash outside, I did it now I'm in the exit but my car was hitting the walls left and right, my rear tires burst, sparks were flying from my rims, I hit my head on the left side of the roll cage and my ear piece fell out of my ear, thank god I had the roll cage covered with a protective soft layer, last thing I heard was ruby screaming out my name, I kept my foot on the gas and pushed myself into the seat as hard as I can .

I got to the other end of the exit tunnel almost unconscious, my car is wrecked from front to back both sides, my head was throbbing, I couldn't see straight for a minutes but I won, it took me a minute to come around and try to move my arms and legs, I got the seat harnesses off and pushed the front wind shied to get out of the car, I dragged myself out and stood up, looked back and saw solo coming with a smile on his face, I was so ready to kill this guy right now but I had to hold my self and play it cool, there is more to this game than this race, plus he gave me a 2 reasons to kill him later with no regrets, so I took a few deep breathes and walked a bit to regain my balance, the guy that was waiting at the finish line did nothing to help me get out of the car, he was standing there waiting for solos orders, he put his hand under his jacket like was ready to pull out a gun as solo came closer to me, then he starts to clap and said .

-Solo-congratulations, you won.
-Me-you almost killed me, others would run and hide solo.
-Solo-but you survived, you mess with the bull you get the horns, and you proved yourself worthy to be in my organization, and I had to test how well you can handle yourself under extreme pressure.
-Me-I survived for two reasons, one of them is this partnership.
-Solo-and number two?
-Me-you'll know when the time is right, the question now is, are you going to keep your word or not?
-Solo-welcome to my world DJ, come with me.
-Me-what about my car?

-Solo-if you play your cards right from now on, you'll buy 10 cars better than that old piece of junk.

he doesn't know it but he just gave me one more reason to kill him, nobody calls my baby an old piece of junk, I told him I need a minute to pick up a few things from my car, solo went back to his car and the guy that was at the starting line just arrived with the bus to pick up the lambo, I found my phone but I couldn't find the ear piece, as I was surching I tried to talk to ruby quietly.

-Me-ruby are you there, I lost my ear piece, I can't hear you guys, if you can hear me don't worry I'm ok, a bit banged up but mostly ok, hit me up with some power, fighting skills and speed, I hope the contact lenses still work you need to see where I'm going with this guy ok keep tracking me,and please send someone to pick up my baby, don't leave it here until morning, peace for now .

few seconds later I got the shiver I knew they got my message, I walked back to where solo was, I called home coz I didn't want the family to worry about me, told them that I'll be back by tomorrow maybe coz I'm going to attend a race event in another state and I got everything I need with me, solo heard it all and as we got in the bus he said.

-Solo-still a mama's boy ha?
-Me-it's called family, people you need to take care of and they take care of you.
-solo-I wouldn't know, I was raised in an orphanage, never knew my family, even in the army the team was the closest thing to a family I had, even then you keep losing members of your team in some missions, so I stopped allowing myself to get emotionally attached to any one, buckle up DJ this going to be a fast ride.
-Me-how fast can it be, it's just a bus.
-Solo-there is more to this bus than what you see, ok boys take us home.

that bus was amazing it had everything you want in a home all that it's missing is a swimming pool, I heard a sound that you would normally hear from a jet engine of an air plane, I can feel the bus lifting, I looked out of the window and I saw that we were off the ground, this bus can take off vertically, then Solo said close the window and hold on DJ, then I felt this crazy boost, this bus just went air born, I looked out and saw what looked like jet engines on the side of the bus that lit with a blue light, I don't know where they came from and this thing was zooming like lightning, then solo started talking about this bus how fast it is and the out of this world technology that it has, undetectable by raider and all that, a minute later he handed me an ice pack to use for the bump on my head .

the trip was about an hour long, I had a snack and we talked about our cars and the new production idea of Slip Dream, it turns out that solo was getting the formula legalized to be used to produce a soft drink, so you can imagine how humans are going to be if this happens, an all you can eat buffet for the aliens, and as he said that Mr. Dean has served his purpose in the process,then he said that the paper work will be ready by the time we get to where we are going, and someone will take a look at my head injury, we arrived at our destination which was in the middle of nowhere.
the bus touched ground on a dark narrow street then we took a right turn on to a dirt road which lead to a farm, all I can see was trees and mountains, the driver pulled up to the mail box and inserted a card in it, then the barn gate opened up and we drove in side, the gate closed and I felt we were on an elevator going down, all I can see was blue neon lights as we went down, I counted about 20 more or less, about 30 seconds later it stopped, and I asked the classic question …

-Me-are we there yet?
-Solo-just a few more minutes.

we were driving in a tunnel that took us into the mountain behind the farm, the tunnel was well built, it looked like a long glass tube, I can see rocks and there were places where the tube was just suspended in air, we passed through underground caves, I can see that we were deep underground by now and the best part is that I can see it all coz the place was lit throughout the rout, it was like a journey to the center of the earth, I was looking out of the windows like a little kid, we started to slow downwhen we reached a huge gate with strange symbolic writings on it, seconds later the gate opened and we drove into what looked like a city built inside the mountain .

we got out of the bus and solo took me inside, the first thing that caught
my eye was a huge dark red crystal that was hanging from above, that
rock was as big as cruise ship and was glowing green, it looked like an
underwater world but without water, It felt like being on another planet, as
we walked inside solo started to explain some of the things I was looking
at, I saw levels all around like a shopping mall, aliens going back and forth
between them hovering around on crystal plates, we got into an elevator
and went up the same way, no cables just a round glass tube to protect us
from falling, about twenty floors later there was a Japanese theme garden,
it was the whole deal with the bamboo plants and trees, a coy fish pond
with a bridge that goes over it that lead into a Japanese style home with the
paper doors, inside was a state of art home .

-Solo-welcome to my house DJ, the kitchen is there, the guests bedroom
is there, you'll find some clean clothes in the closet and warm food in the
kitchen, make your self at home.
-Me-very nice, I'm really impressed.
-Solo-glad you like it, I'll be back in a little while.

then he went outside, I looked around the place it had that Feng shui
thing going on, this is what a real home should feel like, I took a shower
coz I was smelling like hot sauce and fuel, I looked in the mirror to check
if the contact lens was still there, I took it out and I saw that it was torn
a bit maybe coz of the head bang I got, thank god coz I was worried that
something went wrong with my eye, I had a nice meal after the shower then
I timed my phone to ring in an hour coz I needed to take a nap, after an
hour I woke up feeling fresh, and still there was no sign of solo, I thought
I'd take a look around this place, I was just about to open the door when
solo came in .

-Solo-I see that you feel better, did you get some rest?
-Me-yea but my head still hurts a bit.
-Solo-come on let's get you checked out.

we got on to the elevator and went down, I kept looking outside at the city,
I couldn't believe what my eyes are seeing, this alien race has turned this
place to what looked like how they lived at their home planet, there were
little baby aliens and adults, this race is thriving here, even the trees and

plants they had looked weird, there were cocoon shaped mega structures with bubble glass, some of it was carved in the mountain others were hanging in midair, they are using anti-gravity technology and some of the structures are connected to each other by bridges hanging high above the ground.

there was a stream flowing between all the structures, looks like it's carrying information through some kind of energy cables, and all that energy flows from and to the giant red crystal, we got out of the elevator to what solo called the science level, where he said will get my injury healed, there is something about this place, the energy that flows through it that makes you feel rejuvenated and energized, I think it's because of the red crystal that stores and spreads out the energy in this place, makes you feel like you can never get sick or tired or even grow old, maybe that's the reason why solo looks the way he is now,I was looking at all that's around me and I started to forget why I came here in the first place, my god it's huge, and so many aliens moving all around it .

-Solo-DJ you have to know that we are dealing with beings that are out of this world.
-Me-what do you mean? (I had to pretend that I don't know what he was talking about)
-solo-all what you see here is alien technology, all these people you see here are aliens in human form, they are beings of energy and they cultivate our bioenergy to live, they don't eat or drink normal food, they take some of our energy and in return the will give us almost unlimited knowledge and technology .

we entered what looked like a healing room and I acted like I'm super surprised, a lady doctor came and used a device that I have never seen before to check my head, and the image of my injury came up on a screen in midair in front of us, I'm looking at my brain functions right in front of me, she said that it's not bad and it would heal over a short period of time, but they will enhance the healing process to make it heal in a few minutes, I had to see this for myself, so I said please do it, the doctor rubbed her hands together and a bright green light started to shine through her fingers, then she stood next to me and asked me to close my eyes, I felt a comforting worm sensation where my injury was, I felt her hand moving in a circular motion, it was so comforting I almost fell asleep for a minute, I opened my eyes and looked in the mirror and the bump was gone, like it never was there .

-Solo-how do you feel?
-Me-I feel good, I don't believe what just happened.
-Solo-there is more to this alien race than you can imagine, come on we have one more stop then I'll show you how they make our magic potion.

we got out and solo was telling me about how great it would be to have these aliens share this planet with us and share their technology with us to make our country the most advanced country on the planet, the guy was brain washing me with his words, his point of view started to appeal to me in a weird way, he brought up Atlas and how they hunted down these aliens before he understood the benefits of having them on our side and atlas didn't see things his way and tried to have him arrested and put in jail, he escaped and collaborated with gangsters at first to make this dream of his see the light, and after the invasion of the headquarters the gangsters turned on him, they wanted it all for themselves, after he took most of them down he had the idea of getting this drug legalized and sell it as a new beverage, that's why he worked with Mr. Dean through his medical company it was easier to make this drug legal.

but Mr. Dean has served his purpose and he is out of the equation now, and after Mr. Deans death some of the labs that produced the drug were raided and closed or burned to the ground, some of the workers got arrested others died, so solo decided to bring the production in here, and because they lost huge amount of weed in the raids, they needed a supplier and that's where I come in .

I saw some of the aliens in their true form, they stand upright like us, 2 hands 2 legs no mouth 2 golden eyes, a form of almost transparent greenish body, a kind of bioenergy contained in a human shaped cast, they looked like Casper the friendly ghost but with legs, solo told me that they are slowly changing shape to take human form and live among us in the outside world, and when they move the just float like an inch above ground, they wear synthetic skin to look like humans and blend in, they are peaceful as solo explained, they only want to coexist and share this planet with us .

after they lost their planet and came to earth many years ago, most of them were in deep hibernation to conserve what little energy they had left, and at first the aliens didn't understand how fragile earth system is, they caused some major problems like droughts and famines across the globe coz they were hungry for energy to revive their own kind, so they took whatever they can grab, but after a while of studying our planet and examining life forms that live on it they got to know us better and knew what they exactly needed .

we stopped at one place and solo looked into my eyes and asked me to make the call, set up an appointment to get the weed here and keep the production going, and prepare myself for a new world with all that I want at my fingertips, then he said he'll be back in a minute .

I found myself thinking about all what solo told me, my mind was leaning towards what he said but my heart wasn't, I kept looking around like a lost kid, looking for an answer, I put my hand in my pocket and pulled out the phone and the battery was dead, then I though what if we have no more energy, what if they drained humanity out, these aliens could have done this to other planets before us, I looked back to see where solo is and I saw the two chicks that almost killed Darrell talking to him behind the glass, then it all came back to me, it flashed in my head, the videos that atlas showed me, my brother fighting for his life in my arms, the race and how solo almost killed me and wrecked my car, and he had the nerve to call my baby a piece of junk, it brought the fire inside me back to life again .

I couldn't take my eyes of them, then I started to hear what they were talking about, thank you atlas for the nanobots, I heard the girls tell solo that what he was waiting for is almost ready, they just need a drop of blood from solo so it would lock on to his D.N.A, and she was pointing at a huge greenish chrome egg with tubes and wires connected to it, what is in that giant egg ??, one of them tuned at me and said to solo that I look familiar and solo told them that they can have me when he got the weed I have, coz after that he has no need for me what so ever, solos arrogance is going to get him killed sooner than he knows, my emotions were taking over me to the point that I'm having tunnel vision, I can see these three persons and nothing else, at this moment I'm barely keeping my face straight both my hand are tight fists, and I realized that I'm in the right place at the right time with all the reasons that I need to do what I'm about to do .

last thing I remember after that time was looking at solo and girls and one of them was giving me dirty looks while the other one was trying to get a blood sample from solo as I walked towards them, then my brain went blanc, moments later I heard an emergency siren, one of the girls had called for help coz I came into the lab and instead of flirting with her friend I used her as punching bag and solo jumped me in her defense and I started fighting with him, and wrecking everything in that lab and the girl couldn't get his blood sample, she dropped whatever she was doing and rushed to her friend to see if she was ok, solo and I were having a hell of a fight, turns out that solo has had some upgrades of his own thanks to his alien allies, he can stand up to my strength, speed, and fighting skills .

I can see his upgrades showing on his body, blue dots on his spine connect to dark metallic lines that leads to muscles and joints in his arms and legs, I saw that when his shirt got torn off in the fight, I managed to avoid around punch from him but he got me with the round kick that followed it,and it threw me through the dividing glass into the next room, I landed on what looked like a dentist chair, I needed a few seconds to get my head together after that kick, suddenly I felt a needle penetrating the palm of my right hand, I pulled my hand up quick and saw a drop of blood coming out, that system was ready to take solos blood but instead it took mine, nothing to worry about I was a bit banged up already and solo was too, neither of us was gaining or losing ground, the place was almost totaled, almost all the lights were broken, the girls left the lab and left us alone to fight it out between us a long time ago, I couldn't see him but I can hear him so I'm walking around the place looking for him very carefully, then I heard him say
-Solo-why are you doing this DJ
-Me- this is my fight, for what those two bitches did to my brother, for what these aliens are about to do to our world, coz you tried to killed me when I won the race, and for calling my baby a piece of junk.
-Solo-who sent you?
-Me-I came by myself, I don't work for nobody.
-Solo-I don't believe you, I think Atlas sent you.

-Me-as I said this is my fight, I don't work for Atlas, and you're invited to get a 5 star ass whopping.

-Solo- DJ if we play our cards right they can make this a better world for all of us, forget what Atlas told you, we can live like kings for the rest of our lives .

-Me-do you really believe that shit, just coz they made you a few years younger, gave you some upgrades and some money, you must be out of your god damn mind solo, all they will do is suck our world dry and humanity will vanish coz of stupid greedy people who think that these aliens will give them eternal life, riches and power, if they gave it to you they can take it back just as easy, now come out here and let me kick your ass like a gentleman .

-Solo-don't make me do this DJ.

-Me-do your worst bitch.

I remembered my rings, I had them in my pocket so I put them on, and solo did the same too, I heard footsteps coming in the place, there was more of us in the place not just solo and me, they were the alien security, in human form with laser guns and solo was directing them while he was talking to me to circle me in a corner so they can take me out, I kept hearing weird sounds after that needle took some of my blood, I saw solos reflection on a piece of broken glass on the floor, he was hiding behind a big box not too far away from me, but I couldn't see the alien security that he was talking to, until I looked up, these guys were actually walking upside down on the ceiling and they were getting close to where I was .

I'm cornered, I heard something crack open behind me in the dark part of the room, like a pressure pod then I kept hearing a sound of trapped air leaking, seconds later it faded away and I saw white smoke floating on the floor coming from behind me, I need to get out of this corner and escape outside to have a better chance to defend myself, then (solo said ready or not her we come), the best thing I can do was to get down on one knee and shield myself with the rings, the fire power was too much for one person to handle, solo and these guys were making it rain like hell on me, I felt a slimy thing crawling on my leg, I turned to check what it was and it pulled me back so hard and fast into the dark part of the lab, I was screaming my head off, I thought that this was some alien monster trying to eat me or something, solo and the security stopped firing and they were listing to me screaming my head off in the darkness.

I felt these wet cold tentacles tearing off my clothes and wrapping around my hands and legs holding me upright, I felt one of them stuck on my spine from the back of my neck all the way down, needles penetrating my skin going into my spine, there was some pain at first then my body went numb, no more pain, I'm not screaming anymore, these tentacles kept on wrapping around my whole body, suddenly I'm not afraid anymore, whatever this thing is it's starting to feel so natural and familiar to me, like a warm and soothing hug from an old friend, it took over me, I felt it connecting to everything inside me and we are becoming as one,it even bonded with the nanobots and the rings,I can hear solo calling my name while he and the team were coming closer, I can hear his voice echoing as if I was dreaming, I was in a cocoon that's starting to take the shape of my body .

I lived that sensation for a minute then I opened my eyes to find myself standing on my feet, I looked at my hands and my body and saw my self-covered from head to toe in a body armor that's made from something that I have never seen before, it feels light organic and alive, I never felt so alive and full of energy, reborn into a new me, and I can see clearly in the dark, ok let's see what this armor can do, time to play, smoke filled the room that I was in, I'm walking out, all they heard was the sound of compressed air being released and saw a pair of angry silver eyes coming at them, they all froze trying to figure out what is this thing standing in front of them .

-Solo-are you in there DJ?
-Me-yep.
-Solo-you know that this power armor is mine right?
-me- so that's what it is, well I got news for you, finders keepers, it's mine now, come and get it if dare.

I guess solo started boiling on the inside coz he didn't say anything he just started shooting and screaming, so we're back to where we started, extensive fire power, everybody was shooting at me again, I jumped back when they started shooting to get some distance between us,now I have shield in one hand and a gun in the other, I'm shooting and moving until I found a way out to some more open space, now here is where the real fun started, I can maneuver like crazy, now I can see everyone who's shooting at me, I still didn't have it in me to kill so I'm injuring them just enough to stop shooting, the weird thing was that when ever I shoot one of the alies the the synthetic skin and clothes fall on the ground and a green ball of energy floates up and get absorbed into the giant red crystal, I managed to stop the security team that was with solo and now it's just me and him on a bridge hanging high between the cocoons .

-Solo-I can't believe you took my armor, how does it feel in there?
-Me-feels great, I can't even begin to describe it, I love the way the helmet opens up.
-Solo-I was waiting for it for more than a year for it, you know they grew this from a seed, and genetically engineered it to become a bio boosted combat machine, full capabilities still unknown, combat abilities almost unlimited, what you have on right now is the most perfect war machine ever created, doesn't need fuel or charging, it lives off any kind of energy around it, I planned to sell this to the government, I was going to test it but now it looks like I got me a test pilot, do you understand what it is to have that kind of technology at the palm of your hands DJ, surly a man as smart as you should see the benefits of collaborating with these aliens by now .

-Me-oh I see it, but the price that they want is too expensive, think years from now, what would happen to this planet, these aliens might have done this to their own planet, drove it to the point where it can't support them anymore, maybe they done this to many other planets before us, god only knows how long these aliens have been doing this, that's why they wonder from one planet to the other just to stay alive, what's next for you solo, have you ever thought of having a family of your own someday, or do you want to wonder the galaxy with them for the rest of your life .

-Solo-that's not your problem, what you should worry about right now is staying alive, what do you say we fight it out the old fashion way, with swords a gentelman's weapon, coz I want my suit back with minimum damage, what do you say to that.
-Me-if that's what you want then so be it, by the way Atlas says hi.
-Solo-I knew it since I saw the laser shield you used, I saw the rings on your fingers, you have the other four right.
-Me-yep, and looking forward to taking the two you have.
-Solo-oh no I'm getting the ones you got, choose your sword.

-Me-let's dance.

solo used the rings to produce a European knight sword, I choose a Japanese samurai katana, I didn't know if I had the skill to fight with this kind of weapon but it sure felt good to try, we are standing there face to face ready to fight, suddenly there were lasers shooting at me, solo was acutely buying himself some time until reinforcements arrive and they did, but this time they were airborne and with bigger guns, solo got distracted for a second giving me all the time I needed to make my move, I ran towards him and chopped his hand off, and jumped off the bridge to catch it and land one of the level below that was the plan, I cough Solo's hand in midair and I got shoot on my way down and knocked my head on the stone wall then fell unconscious all the way down to the ground floor, I finally have the last two ring and they got fused with the armor, the armor had some damage from the shoot but nothing serious, it took a couple of minutes for the alien ground troops to come to the level I was in while the airborne troops were hovering closely, the damage from the shoot was recovering .

then it happened, the eyes of the armor turned red and it went into battle mood all by itself, total annihilation, that baby burned the hell out of them, it showed what it was made for, shoulders caps open to expose mini laser cannons and on the wrists, and one on the head plus using the power of the rings to come up with crazy weapons,I called them mini cannons coz they are small guns that shoot a huge caliber laser shoot, and if that wasn't enough elbow blades appeard cutting down anything that came close, it was shooting down multible targets at the same time, it shoot down the airborne units and cut down the ground team like grass.

They couldn't hit the armor any more it's dodging whatever they throw at it, it's operating on its own, blowing up everything in sight, cutting down almost anything that moves in that place, it simple just went into kill everting mood, it started to climb up cleaning up the place, jumping from one level to the next, then the ground started trembling, the place was falling apart the mothership was detaching from the mountain and whoever was alive went in it, turns out that the top part of the mountain was the camouflaged mothership.

the armor was climbing up to get to the ship before this huge gate closes between the ship and whatever that's below, when the armor saw that, two wings with boosters came out from the back shoulders and calves, how awesome is that, it can fly too, the ship broke off the mountain and the ships massive engines started, the thrust of the engines pushed down so hard that the boosters couldn't take the armor any higher, it actually pushed it back to the ground outside the mountain, I opened my eyes and saw the ship taking off on its way out of the atmosphere.

I wasn't fully awake, I thought I was dreaming at the time and the armor was still in kill mood and it wasn't about to let that ship leave in one piece, it stood up and zoomed on the ship, I started to see energy level gauges in front of my eyes and other stuff I didn't understand, but I can see it was going to do something big, there was a countdown going on in weird numbers and all the gauges levels are moving up, the ship was almost at the edge of space, the armor stood like a cannon, one leg in front of the other, knee bent forward and dug it's feet firmly in the ground, chest aiming high at the ship, arms fully stretched forward, palms facing each other, then the chest plates went down, and an energy build up was happening there, the countdown stopped and all the levels are at the top, I saw a huge energy sphere forming between the palms of my hands, and boom, it shoot 2 of them at the ship, when that happened all levels went down, and it stood up normally chest plates closed and arms down .

the boost of the weapon pushed the armor a few feet back, the spheres kept getting bigger and bigger, moving at twice the speed of sound if not faster, as they got closer to the space ship, the ship was just about to make the jump to light speed, the portal was open and the ship just blasted into light speed and not a second too late the shoots went into the portal just before it closed behind the ship, then I saw a sparkle high up far away in the night sky, I don't know if it was an explosion or was it the morning star .

The place was quite and still dark, and I don't know where the hell I am!, I can't fly back randomly, I remembered that I had my phone with me when the armor took over me, I thought why not so I said call ruby, and it did, it even connected to my phone, a few rings and she picked up, she sounded really worried .

-Ruby-papi are you ok, we couldn't see where you were all night, where are you.

-me-I'm ok sweet cheeks, I don't know where I am can you send me a location so I can follow it back.

-Ruby-sure papi, what happened, all of us were worried sick.

-Atlas-hey DJ, I'm glad you're still in one piece.

-Me-yea me too.

-Atlas-come on back we have a lot to talk about in full detail.

-Me-yea sure, by the way did you guys pick up my car?

-Atlas-it's parked outside your workshop.

-Me-how bad is the damage?

-Atlas-how would I know, I'm not your god damn mechanic, get your butt over here ASAP.

-Me-I'll see you when I see you guys, thanks for taking care of my baby, peace for now.

I hung up and I got the location, I looked in the palm of my hand and a screen display lit up in front of me, I was shocked to know that I was in the mid-west, I'm a long way from home, my other problem was how to make this armor fly, it took a few tries to get the wings and boosters out, then came the flying part, clumsy at first, almost hit the side of the barn, but I learned along the way back, I loved the ultra-high speed part, all I have to do is think about what I want it to do and it does it, sweet god I think I traveled back in time that's how fast it was, the best part was flying at high speed between buildings in the city, I might have shattered a few window on the way but it was worth it, I got to my house and landed in our back yard, now for the last part of this nights adventure, how to get out of this battle armor, the one thing that solo didn't tell me.

I tried lots of ways but nothing worked, I only got as far as getting the mask of my face, then it hit me, it came to me when I needed it, so if I can tell it that I'm safe and secure maybe it will leave me coz I wouldn't know how to explain this to my parents if they saw it, I have to do this and I have to do it fast, I focused on one idea, i closed my eyes and kept saying in my head I'm safe and secure over and over again, then the magic happened, it just floated off me like a silver shadow and kept going higher and higher into the night sky until it disappeared, I watched it go with a smile and a tear in my eye, I looked down and saw that I'm wearing nothing but my underwear and found a tattoo on the inner side of my right forearm, it was a crescent facing right with a small drawing of Saturn in the middle of it, I rushed inside before the neighbors see me like this, I felt like a part of me left with the armor.

Now I needed 3 things, first a shower, second eat and thierd sleep in my bed, a new day is about to begin, what more surprises could it have for me, I went to sleep around 6 am and woke up at 2 pm,i had brunch and went out, I got me a new phone then passed by the workshop and brought my car inside,i checked it out, my baby needs a lot of TLC to get it back in shape, I got a few things done, then later I went to see Atlas and Ruby, they did a full medical check on me and found that I'm in good shape but I only have 5% of the nanobots left in my body and a strange subsistence in my blood and other stuff they said about my cells that I didn't understand, but I was in good health and that's what's important.

I told them everything that happened since I got out of the car crash and what I saw inside the mountain until the part where I got shoot and fainted and woke up to find my self outside the mountain and the armor shooting at the alien ship, i showed them the tattoo and the doctor examined it and said that the tattoo is burned on my skin, atlas wanted to see the armor but for some reason I couldn't make it happen, maybe I was in a very good mood at the time, Atlas asked me about the rings and I told him that they were infused with the armor, I left the base and drove by amber's bakery, I just had to know, she took my hand and put it on her tummy, she looked in my eyes and smiled, and I was shoot into another dimension, I saw the next phase of my life in her blue eyes, and I couldn't wait to live that adventure, and moms wish finally came true, Atlas kept his word to Mr.Dean and moved him to a special prison where he can see the sun and other people.

Meanwhile somewhere on Saturn's biggest moon Titan, inside a cave there is a beautiful green garden with the most exotic weird plants and small creatures that you can ever imagine, lives an enchanting oracle wearing a necklace with a pendant that looks like the tattoo on my forearm, the crescent with Saturn in the middle of it, but the piece that represents Saturn is an indigo pearl that started to glow, the oracle looked into it and saw the image of the bio-boosted armor floating inside, she smiled then said.
-Oracle- finally the seed was planted and new galactic assassin is born.

============== The End ============

===========================

A litte about me, I've been in quite a few shoes in my life like,sports, party and radio and dj, i have a deploma in automotive mechanics,a hypnotherapy practitioner, and now novel writing, and that is just some of many, i try to keep an open mind and i learn new things as i go, lately i found out that writing is in the top four of my missions in life list,i never thought that i can ever write a novel in my life but here we are with my first one, it took around three years for this novel to come to your hands,i personally thank you for buying this novel and I hope that you enjoyed reading it.
words of advice, never limit your self and explore new horizons you never know what you can achieve.

yours respectfuly

Ahmed Alnajem d(o_-)b

(A-star@hotmail.com)

Printed in the United States
By Bookmasters